The Monsters Are Coming

Brill Harper

Published by Brill Harper, 2024.

This is a work of fiction. Similarities to real people, places, or events are entirely coincidental.

THE MONSTERS ARE COMING

First edition. March 9, 2024.

Copyright © 2024 Brill Harper.

ISBN: 979-8224682751

Written by Brill Harper.

The Wolf of Wallace Woods

THE WOLF OF WALLACE Woods is a local legend that terrifies everyone in town. Everyone except for Paige. She dreams about the werewolf at night, waking up hot and bothered and yearning. But she doesn't really believe in him. Not until the creature is actually chasing her through the forest. Not until he's caught her. Not until he growls the only word he knows: **Breed**.

Chapter One

THE LEGEND OF THE WOLF of Wallace Woods has kept the locals entertained and the tourists terrified for over a century. Much like a Sasquatch sighting, the wolf is much talked about but never seen.

I read plenty of shifter romance novels, but *this* wolf is not like *those* wolves. At least according to the legends. He's not a pack animal, for one thing.

He's an eerie, solitary figure, a specter that roams the gloomy depths of the Wallace Woods seeking no companionship, finding solace only in the lullaby of the wind and the symphony of nocturnal creatures. This wolf is far from amicable; he's a manifestation of pure fear and primal instinct. He's a rogue. A loner. A creature of the night, shrouded in mystery and terror.

And sometimes I dream about him.

In my dreams, I'm traversing the sinuous paths of Wallace Woods, a silvery moon bathing the underbelly of the forest in an ethereal glow. My skin prickles with expectation. Then there he is.

The Wolf of Wallace Woods emerges from the eerie murk cloaked in an unearthly aura that hums with predatory prowess. He's larger, more formidable than the most fearsome beast of nature's design. His eyes, an incandescent blend of molten gold and fiery amber, are fixed on me, glowing under the spectral moonlight. They hold a crushing intensity, a ferocious hunger that makes my blood run cold. Yet, of all the emotions that spill from his feral eyes, it's the intense loneliness that clings to me the most, lingers on in the recesses of my mind even after I've woken up.

Legend says he can walk upright like a man using his front paws like hands. But when he runs, it's on all fours, fast as the lightning that splits the midnight sky, silent as the falling snow on the frosted grounds.

In my dreams, I run.

And he likes it.

In the cold light of waking, I can always feel the adrenaline pumping through me, my heart pounding like a wild drum. My lucid dreams often leave me unnerved with a lingering sense of dread that is hard to shake off.

And the fact that I'm really, really wet.

My bedside drawer has a toy that I only use when I wake up from *those* dreams. I can't even look at the abomination the rest of the time. It's a novelty dildo made by a company that specializes in monster and sci-fi dicks.

This particular one is designed to mimic the phallus of a creature not governed by any law of physics, a creature like the werewolf that haunts my dreams. Modeled with meticulous attention to details, it has an intimidating size and shape and a "realistic" texture complete with ridges and veins that add an edge of authenticity. I mean, as authentic as you can get with werewolf peen.

It also has a knot. And that's the part that fascinates me.

The large knot is at the base and not something I've ever been able to actually accommodate. I'm ashamed to say that I have tried. It's just too big. I mean, the fact that I can get the rest of the dildo inside me is crazy and fucked up anyway. It didn't happen the first time. The first few times even. I've had to train like some kind of pussy athlete. But the knot is still too much. No matter how much I fantasize about taking it.

There is something very wrong with me for being so interested in it, I think.

In some of the books I've read, the shifter or alpha knot doesn't expand until the cock is already inside the character's pussy, anyway. It's not just hanging out at the base of the cock like it is on the dildo. The knot is how the beast keeps the woman still; the bulge acting as a kind of plug while he finishes his task. It's deeply primal, and deeply disturbing when you really think about it. But in the haze of these lurid dreams, my mind often glosses over the more questionable parts.

The knotting isn't about pleasure; it's about possession. It's about claiming. The knot ensures the seed isn't wasted, that every ounce of the werewolf's essence is poured and sealed within, marking its territory from the inside out. The heroine carries the progeny of the beast, forever marked by the creature. It's all very dark, and yet, I feel very drawn to it.

"Order up."

I blink away my musings as the bell on the counter rings and the cook lets me know that table four's order is ready. That damn dream got me again last night, and I still feel its effects even though I'm at work hours later.

It's the usual rush hour at Maggie's, the cozy diner where I work. I balance the platter of pancakes and bacon on one hand, pouring coffee with the other for Mr. Granger, who takes his breakfast here religiously.

The bell on the door jingles and a man comes in looking like a hunter wearing all his gear. His eyes, a cold shade of blue, are weathered and weary, much like the rest of him. The door creaks shut behind him as he strides to the counter and sits down on a worn, red vinyl stool. The hunter's gaze rolls over the diner, taking in the regulars. He orders black coffee and sits hunched over the counter, his hands cradling the warm ceramic mug.

The door jingles again and Dr. Rain Stockard comes in. We don't see much of Dr. Stockard in town. He's some sort of reclusive professor living deep in Wallace Woods. On sabbatical maybe?

He's not conventionally handsome, though plenty of women would jump at the chance to be noticed by him. He carries with him a mysterious aura, an uncanny intelligence. There is almost as much speculation about Dr. Stockard as there is about the Wolf.

He doesn't fit in very well and doesn't try to. He sticks to his remote cabin and his research. I don't know what he's studying other than it's not the sociology of small town living, obviously.

He takes a seat in the window, and as I'm grabbing the coffeepot and a menu, I see the hunter get up and join him.

Interesting.

They look intense, and I don't want to disturb them, but it's sort of my job.

Taking a deep breath, I weave my way through the narrow passages between tables and chairs until I'm standing right next to their table. There's an electric tension in the air around them that turns the warm ambiance of the diner into something colder, harder.

"Good morning, gentlemen."

I take their orders and leave them to whatever conspiracy, or rivalry, or whatever has drawn these two strange figures to share a table at Maggie's on this otherwise ordinary morning.

Old Mr. Granger grunts from his corner for a top off on his coffee, and I move away from the two men hastily, grateful for the distraction. But as I pour another steaming cup for my regular, I can't help but steal glances at the hunter and the professor seated together. They talk in hushed tones, gruff murmurings from the hunter complemented by low, measured responses from the professor. Their conversation seems cloaked in its own private language.

When I bring their food, the hunter asks me if I've ever seen the wolf.

I chuckle. That's what this is about? Honestly. Two grown men, one a scholar, are talking about werewolves?

"No," I reply, trying to suppress my smile. "I can't say that I have."

The professor doesn't look up from his plate, but the hunter watches me with piercing blue eyes. There's a hint of amusement in them, a glint of something that makes me think he might know more than he's letting on.

Chapter Two

LATER THAT EVENING

My windshield wipers are stuck. That's the first thing I notice when I wake up. As I sit in my car, rubbing at the already forming goose egg on my forehead, I realize that I have to get out of my car. It's not safe to stay in it. I must have been in an accident? The details aren't clear, my memory foggy. But I'm in a ditch at a bad angle, and I won't be simply backing out to get back on the road. The engine is stalled, but my radio is still playing.

As I'm trying to open the car door, not an easy task because of the angle of my car, bits and pieces come back to me. The song on the radio is the same I'd been singing to when I saw something in the road, so I haven't been unconscious for more than a minute. What did I see?

I crawl out of my car, trying to pick up the string of events that led to my current predicament. The moonlight of the full moon washes over the scene, casting elongated shadows that stretch across the road. I walk back toward the spot where it all happened, my shoes crunching on the gravely roadside.

In the eerie quiet of night, I squint to identify any unusual shapes or movements. My heartbeat thrums too loudly in my ears. My hands shake as I point my phone at the sky trying to find service even though I know it's pointless. This part of the highway is always a dead zone.

I shiver. Suddenly "dead zone" sounds much, much more ominous.

My gaze falls on a patch of darkened asphalt—the place where I swerved. Breath clings in my throat as I take hesitant steps forward, my mind darting between fear and morbid curiosity.

The moon, hanging like a silver coin in the ink-black sky, illuminates a spot of something on the asphalt. I lean over, squinting at the patch of liquid. It's blackish, but I can't be certain if it's oil or...blood.

Suddenly, a low growl from behind me snaps my attention. I startle, jerking around to face the source of the noise. My heart jumps into my throat as a figure detaches itself from the gloom, long and lanky like an extra tall man, yet with an animalistic saunter that sets my hairs on end. It steps into the moonlight, revealing a creature unlike any I've seen before—a grotesque blend of man and beast. He's muscular and human-ish. But covered in dark fur.

Its face is an unsettling mixture of human and lupine features, a snout-like nose and pointed ears standing out above uncannily expressive eyes. Those eyes glint in the moonlight with malevolent intelligence. It bares its teeth in what seems like an approximation of a smile, sharp canines glinting threateningly.

So I run.

The crunch of gravel beneath my shoes echoes in harmony with the pounding of my heart. I risk a backward glance and see the creature loping after me, its long strides covering ground rapidly. It opens its maw and howls, a lament that shatters the peace of the night and freezes the blood in my veins.

Fuckity fuck fuck fuck.

Fear is a potent motivator, and I somehow find the strength to push my legs faster, to weave through the labyrinthine trees and overgrown foliage as though my life depends on it—because it does.

And I run until the creature leaps in front of me.

The beast snarls, a guttural sound that vibrates through the air and sends tremors of terror down my spine. It pauses for a second, nostrils flaring as though tasting the air before advancing toward me with a predator's certainty.

As the distance between us dwindles, my mind whirls in a chaotic dance of terror and desperation. My eyes dart around frenziedly for any potential saviors, only to be met by the unforgiving wilderness.

Terror is a thick paste in my mouth, bitter and relentless, as I back up against the thick trunk of a towering tree. The creature moves closer, saliva dripping from its elongated jaws. Its eyes lock onto mine, carrying a terrifying mix of animal desire and human comprehension. I am paralyzed, trapped in its hypnotic gaze.

"Please," I beg.

He puts his muzzle in my neck and huffs.

His breath is hot, humid, permeating my skin with a sense of imminent threat. I can feel each sharp tooth hovering over the fragile expanse of my throat, the threat of savagery unmistakable. He pulls back slightly, and for a terrifying moment, I think it's the end for me.

Instead, he licks the side of my face. The action is so startling that I can't suppress a gasp. It's almost tender. *Almost.*

The creature's eyes keep mine captured, revealing an unsettling intelligence. Is there a man inside the beast? How much of him is left?

His eyes narrow, and he grabs my wrist in his surprisingly humanlike paw. His grip is ironclad, and despite all the adrenaline coursing through me, I can't break free.

He drags me over his shoulder and spirits me away through the forest, the ground beneath us a blur. The landscape is a whirlwind of green and brown, occasionally interspersed with the flash of a fleeing animal or the glint of moonlight piercing the dense canopy above. The creature's pace is unyielding, unaffected by the harsh terrain or my futile attempts to get free.

The forest seems to stretch on endlessly. My heart thunders in time with the crunching leaves beneath his feet, each beat reminding me of my impending fate. There is no mercy in his movements, no sign that he's aware of my protests aside from an occasional irritated growl.

As we forge relentlessly through the forest, a strange calm envelops me, the fear replaced by an unexpected acceptance. What choice do I have but to submit to my fate? This is how I die then. Very well, let's get on with it.

He slows, coming to a stop in a clear, moonlit glen and sets me down and howls again. His preternatural gaze lands on me and I think he speaks.

It sounds like he says, "Breed."

Chapter Three

OH, HELL NO.

I take off to run again, but he catches me easily. His hand..paw...whatever spanning my womb.

He growls again, the inhuman sound reverberating around the glen. I can't help but flinch at the raw power of his voice, the overwhelming sense of dominance that he seems to exude so effortlessly.

"I am not breeding with a werewolf," I tell him, unsure where this last bit of sass comes from.

He looks at me, one ear flicking in what I can only interpret as surprise. The silver moonlight illuminates his sharp features, accentuating the otherworldly, beastly exterior. His golden eyes narrow and he tilts his head, a low growl rumbling deep in his chest.

I'm not as scared as I should be.

In fact, now that we stopped running, I feel something else more unwelcome than fear.

I'm such a pervert.

Fuckity fuck fuck fuck.

Maybe, hopefully, I'm still dreaming. Because I cannot seriously be trapped in the forest with the Werewolf of Wallace Woods and getting wet from the word *breed*.

In my dreams of the werewolf, I never did anything sexual with the beast. I just woke up horny. And in need of my monster dildo. My eyes involuntarily slide down his body to where his cock is, and my breath hitches. If I'm not dreaming, things are about to get very wild, very quickly.

Outrageously, he seems to notice my glance, a growl rippling from him, low and sensual. I quickly tear my gaze away, red heating my cheeks despite the crisp night air.

The werewolf takes a step towards me, the muscles beneath his fur moving with a grace that belies his size. His nostrils flare as if he can sense my sudden and unwelcome arousal—hell, maybe he can—and something in his eyes flares with heat. I take an involuntary step back, my heart pounding in my chest. The werewolf doesn't slow his approach, though, and I soon find my back pressed against a towering oak, the damp moss cushioning my back as my legs go weak.

He snarls, taking my blouse in his razor-sharp teeth and with a swift jerk, rips it open. Cool night air kisses my exposed skin, goosebumps rising in its wake. His golden eyes trail over my body, hunger and desire flaring in their depths. I can't move, caught in his gaze like a deer in headlights.

No flight. No fight. All freeze.

My bra is next to go, the delicate lace offering no resistance against his sharp canines. I gasp as the chill of the night air hardens my nipples. He pauses, eyes drinking in the sight of my bare chest.

How much man is in this beast?

His snout nudges against my breast, hot breath sending my nerves skittering, his golden eyes pinning my gaze to him. He growls again, the sound vibrating against my skin, causing a spike of arousal that I can't ignore. His teeth graze lightly over my nipple, and I gasp at the unexpected sensation. His tongue slides out, rough against the sensitive peak, and another moan rips from my throat.

He pushes me down to my knees and there it is.

His werewolf cock is eerily similar to the novelty werewolf dildo in my bedside drawer. The obscene length and girth glistening in the moonlight. I choke back a gasp of surprise. The cold, hard reality of what's happening to me is finally sinking in.

Everything happens in slow motion: his paw guiding me closer, my hesitant yet intrigued touch, the indecent growl purring from his throat as I explore his member. The texture is rougher than a human, with veins that are more pronounced and ridges that feel almost foreign. The small puddle of pre-cum already forming at his tip looks creamier than a human's.

He groans, low and guttural when I lightly trace one of the prominent veins with a hesitant finger. The sound goes straight to my core, a shiver of anticipation winding its way through my body. I swallow hard, the fear that had been coiling in my stomach now replaced with a growing need I'm familiar with.

The need that always sends me to that damn monster dildo in my drawer.

He urges me closer. His growing impatience is clear in the furious snarl that reverberates deep in his chest, making my heart race and stirring the heat between my legs.

He watches me, his golden eyes glowing intensely under the moonlight, the sinews of his body taut with expectation. He pushes his cock closer to my face, the salty, musky scent of him filling my senses.

My tongue darts out to taste him, and the flavor is overpoweringly male, wild and exotic. A low growl of approval rumbles deep within him, encouraging me to continue my exploration. His cock twitches against my tongue as I lap at the pre-cum pooling at his tip. His taste is a heady mix of musk and the raw tang of wilderness, making me whimper in the back of my throat.

He nudges more insistently now for me to proceed. I tentatively slide my lips over the tapered crown, the velvety texture rubbing against my tongue. He groans deeper this time, the vibration of his pleasure sending a pulse of desire through me. His grip on my hair tightens, the sharp sting bringing a gasp up from my throat. I adjust to his size, his rough texture filling my mouth. His growl of pleasure resounds in the quiet night, the sound making heat bloom in my lower belly.

Roughly, he pulls me back up and makes easy work of my jeans, shredding them in his urgency. His paws are rough and calloused, creating a stark contrast to the softness of my skin. The hiss that escapes my lips is quickly swallowed by the muggy night air, borne away by the whisper of the wind through the surrounding trees.

He pushes me down to my hands and knees.

"Breed," is the only word I've heard him say, and he utters it again in an inhuman voice that is more growl than speech. His voice wraps around me, a primal command that reverberates through each inch of my being.

"No," I squeak.

And then his monster tongue is lapping at me from behind, the unexpected sensation drawing a wheeze from my lungs. His tongue is hot and rough, dragging across the most intimate part of me. The growl that vibrates from his chest is a pure, bestial sound of satisfaction.

"No?" His voice is low, raspy, a dangerous purr that carries a warning. His breath is hot on my skin, the word sending a shudder of fear mixed with excitement through me.

"Breed," he repeats, his rough paw sliding down my spine, digging into the soft flesh of my ass as he asserts his authority. I'm trembling beneath him, my body instinctively responding to the dominance, the command in his voice.

The rasp of his tongue leaves trails of heat on my skin, each swipe coaxing a desperate whimper from me. His scent surrounds me, wild and intoxicating, making every inch of my body tingle with anticipation.

I feel his weight shift, his broad chest pressing against my back as he leans over me, whispering that single word into my ear once more. "Breed."

I flinch at the sensation, the heat of his breath brushing against my earlobe, the ferocity of his voice making my heart hammer against my chest cavity. His monstrous form engulfs me. He's man. He's beast. He promises dark pleasure and pain in equal measure.

The surrounding forest is silent as if the night creatures themselves are holding their breath in anticipation of what is to come. The deafening silence is broken only by his ragged breathing.

"Wait, please," I say. He pulls back enough for me to roll onto my back. I don't know why I'm asking. I don't know why he's allowing.

I make eye contact with the werewolf and gasp. Just like in my dreams of him, his uncannily human eyes are so very lonely. I reach my hand to the side of his face and stroke his soft fur beneath my trembling fingers. He shivers, a low growl rumbling in his throat, but he doesn't pull away. His eyes continue to hold mine, a powerful intensity burning within.

His gaze is an unfathomable mix of human intelligence and feral desire, an incandescent blend of the two worlds he embodies. His paw finds its place on my hip, his claws grazing the skin. "Breed," he breathes out again, the word no longer holding the harsh dominance of before but a plea, a yearning.

"I'm scared," I admit.

Then he hears something, something my ears don't. His head cocks and he sniffs the air. Suddenly, I'm hauled over his shoulder again and he's running. I hear the crack of a gun and realize he's being hunted. I guess that means I am too.

"Put me down," I beg. "You'll run faster on four legs."

I'm certain he understands, but he doesn't comply. We plunge deeper into the forest, the dark foliage a blur as he carries me with supernatural speed. Leaves and branches whip at my face and arms. Another gunshot echoes through the quiet night, closer this time. And yet he runs.

I've not heard other shots for some time when he slows and slides me gently to the ground. We're at a cabin. What is he doing? Someone could see him. He picks me up again, this time bride style, and we go toward the door.

I'm suddenly reminded that I'm completely naked when he kicks the door open. God, he's not going to kill whoever lives here, is he?

He sets me down and then slides to the floor in a heap.

It's then I see the blood.

The Wolf of Wallace Woods has been shot.

Chapter Four

OH MY GOD.

I don't know what else to do other than search for first aid supplies. Anything that will stop the bleeding.

Fuckity. Fuck Fuck Fuck.

The occupants of the house will surely wake up and find us; me naked, him half canine. Why am I not, I don't know, escaping? Waking them up and asking for help? Hitting the werewolf in the head with a fire iron? Anything that resembles self-preservation.

Instead, I find some towels and bandages and tend to the apparently *real* folkloric legend lying unconscious on the wood floor.

He's a werewolf. And I'm not dreaming this time.

The bullet seems to have only grazed him, yet the wound is ugly. Maybe it was a silver bullet, as legends say that is how you kill a werewolf. Maybe the silver is causing the wound to be worse. I don't know what to do for him.

I've cleaned the wound as best I can, so I search the cabin quietly. Despite the fact that there are coals glowing low in the grate, there appears to be no one here. I put on a man's flannel shirt I find hanging on the back of a chair and look for a computer or tablet so I can research how to counter the effects of silver on a werewolf. Notice I'm not looking for vehicle keys or a phone or anything else that will hasten my rescue. There is something very wrong with me.

On the desk, I find a stack of books about...you guessed it. Werewolves. What the actual fuck?

There's a notebook with tightly scribbled thoughts about curses and legends as well. Dawn is breaking when I hear the beast moan. He's waking up. I run to his side to find him convulsing madly.

I don't know what to do or how to help him. I feel so helpless. I don't...what...oh God...he's *changing*.

His body writhes, contorting in ways that seem impossible. I hear the snap of bones shifting and watch in horror as coarse fur recedes, revealing sweat-slicked skin beneath. His features are becoming less bestial and more...human. His hulking form shrinks, a painful metamorphosis that has me reaching out instinctively to soothe him, even as my mind screams at the sheer impossibility of what I'm witnessing.

The creature that has terrified Wallace Woods is no longer a beast, but a man.

His eyes, full of pain, flicker open and latch onto mine. And I recognize him.

"Dr. Stockard?"

"Water," he rasps.

I scramble to find a glass, filling it from the tap and hurrying back to his side. Later. I'll think about all of this later. He tries to sit up to drink, but his body convulses and he falls back, gasping in pain.

"Easy, you're too weak," I murmur, easing my hand beneath his head to lift it slightly as I bring the rim of the glass to his lips. He sips the water greedily, some of it trickling down his chin.

"There's...something in my bag," he rasps out once he's had his fill. He points his head in the direction I'm supposed to look for it.

"To counteract the silver?"

"Pouch."

He nods. I find his bag shoved into a corner and rummage around not sure what I'm even looking for until my hand closes around a small, velvet pouch. The contents jingle with a metallic sound as I rush back to him.

"Pour...it...into water," he manages to instruct, his voice barely a whisper.

I do as he says, tipping the bag's contents into the glass. Tiny flakes of metallic shards float downward, dissolving into the water and turning it a shimmering, iridescent hue. The transformation is mesmerizing, but there's no time to marvel at the spectacle. I hold the glass to his lips once more and he drinks. His body seems to relax almost instantly, the tense lines of pain smoothing out, replaced by an expression of relief and exhaustion. He closes his eyes, his chest rising and falling in a steady rhythm.

"Dr. Stockard? Professor?" I call his name tentatively but he doesn't respond. I watch him for a moment longer, my mind racing to comprehend the events of the past hour. The beast of Wallace Woods, the terror that has haunted our town for generations, is none other than the quiet and reclusive scholar who keeps to himself and his books.

The man I saw at Maggie's Diner just yesterday morning talking to the man who looked like a hunter.

How can that even be right? He's certainly not one hundred plus years old.

"You have questions," he comments.

Now that his color is returning, I'm reminded that Rain Stockard is not only a very handsome man, but that he's also currently a naked one.

"Yes, I do," I reply, blushing and hastily reaching for a nearby throw blanket, covering him with it. "And hopefully you have answers," I add, shifting my gaze from him to the iridescent remnants of the potion in the glass.

"Answers," he echoes, his voice still sounding as brittle as dry leaves, "That depends on the questions. What's your name?" he asks.

"Paige. Paige North. But I think I get to ask the questions from here on out." A million thoughts flood my mind, and I have a hard time deciding where to start. "What are you?" I finally ask, my eyes fixed on his now human form.

"I am a man. A cursed one."

Well, duh.

"HOW WERE YOU CURSED? What exactly is the curse? If you're the Wolf of Wallace Woods, then how old are you?"

He takes another drink, now able to hold the glass himself. "I'm old, but not as old as the legend. The legend used to be just that...a legend...folklore. But I crossed the wrong woman, the wrong witch, and she turned me into the thing I studied."

"You were studying the werewolves?"

He nods. "I was researching the folklore of the werewolves when I met a beautiful woman, and I did poorly by her."

"The witch?"

The professor hangs his head. "I was a very young man and not careful with her heart. She cursed me to become the beast from sundown to sunrise."

"Every night? Not just during the full moon?"

"Unfortunately, every night. The supernatural magic slows my aging process. There is no reprieve from the change, though. I've been searching for a cure ever since. I came to Wallace Woods several years ago to learn what I could about the local legend. To see if it could help me."

"And the witch?"

"She died many years ago, an old woman, taking the remedy to my curse with her to the grave." His eyes, deeply lined with regret and sorrow, meet mine. "Her name was Elara."

I find it hard to breathe. The weight of his revelation is too much. "So you've been searching for a cure for years, and nothing?"

He nods, the desperation in his eyes echoing the sadness in his voice. "Decades. No matter how many potions I've concocted, no matter how many ancient texts I've pored over, nothing has lifted this curse. Only Elara could have undone what she did, but she died before I could make amends."

Sorrow tugs at my heart, and I'm at a loss for words. His despair is tangible, filling the room and seeping into me. The silence that follows is heavy. Broken only by the ticking of an ancient grandfather clock standing sentinel in the corner of the room. I cast my eyes around, looking at the book-laden shelves, the strange, probably ancient, artifacts scattered haphazardly on tables. All testament to his tireless quest for a cure.

"I'm sorry," I finally murmur, my voice barely more than a whisper. "You've been living like this, alone for all these years?"

A wry smile tugs at the corners of his lips. "Isolation tends to come with lycanthropy."

"That hunter that you met with yesterday at the diner. He hunts..."

"Werewolves. Yes. He will kill me if he gets the chance. He almost did."

I shake my head. "Then why did you meet with him if he's your enemy?"

"He doesn't know who I am, that I am the thing he seeks. He only knows me as a scholar of his prey.." The professor stretches carefully. "He might have answers for me. Things I don't know about. His quest is only just the other side of the coin from mine."

"How can you say that? He wants to kill you."

"He wants to kill the beast. As do I. If he has information I can use to break the curse, then I need him. If he learns my secret, he'll kill me, and either way the curse will be broken."

I cannot believe what he is saying. "You can't let him kill you. There has to be another way."

His eyes, filled with the weariness of countless sunsets and moons passed, meet mine once again. "I have tried many paths, numerous spells and rituals, yet here I stand—a man forever chained to his beastly form. Believe me when I say that death is not my preferred outcome, but it is one I have come to accept as a potential resolution."

"Maybe you're missing something," I suggest tentatively, not wanting to disrespect his decades-long efforts but unable to hold back the surge of stubborn optimism that has always been my nature. "Maybe the solution lies in acceptance rather than fighting. In harmony rather than conflict."

He looks at me, a flame flickering in his eyes. Probably a flame of annoyance at my naivety. "Harmony? With the beast? Are you forgetting I almost raped you last night?"

"But you didn't."

Neither of us mention that I was practically in heat for him. Or that he wanted to *breed* me, his beastly instincts overriding any rational thought. But even at the peak of his transformation, he held back. It had been a close call, but he didn't cross that line.

"No, I didn't," he murmurs, looking away. His eyes are haunted as he remembers the fight he waged against his own body just as I remember my own fight against mine.

I've dreamed of the beast. Countless times. Waking up slick and needy. Maybe I'm cursed too.

"How do you know it won't happen next time?" He asks with a bitter twist to his lips, then adds, "Or the time after that?"

"I don't," I reply. "Have you ever...has the beast ever...taken a woman that way?"

He shakes his head. "Raped you mean? No. The beast stays well away from humans every night. I've never felt...that...before. The beast wanted to mate you." He pauses, deep in though. "I should be honest with you, little one. The urges began before sunset. When we were in the diner yesterday, I thought I might change in broad daylight just from your scent. I don't believe you are safe with me. Whether I am a man or beast."

I'm hardly able to process my thoughts when there is a pounding at the door. The professor looks out the window and whispers, "It's Smith. You need to hide in the bedroom."

"Who is Smith?"

"The hunter."

OH MY GOD. THE HUNTER? Here? Now? "Are you insane? I'm not hiding in the bedroom. *You* should hide in the bedroom."

"Paige—"

I point to the bedroom. "Get in the shower or he'll know you've been injured." The wound has healed, but he's still a bloody mess.

Though he's in human form, the professor growls lowly but does as I ask. I stash all the bloody evidence in his oven and open the door a crack. "Yes?"

Mr. Smith, clad in his camouflage and holding a rifle, tries to puzzle out why yesterday's waitress is answering the door. Of Dr. Stockard. "I'm looking for Rain Stockard. I was told he lived here."

If Rain wanted him to know where he lived, they would have met here yesterday, not at Maggie's Diner. I think Smith suspects something about Rain. Why else would he be here, gun in hand? To finish him off is what I'm thinking.

Guess we need to show him he's way off base.

I smile and open the door a little more. "He's in the shower. Hey, I remember you. From the diner yesterday. It's a little early for company...Mr. Smith isn't it?"

He cocks his head, trying to figure out what's going on. "I have important business with Stockard."

"Who's at the door, love?" I hear from behind me. Rain's arm bands around my waist possessively. "Smith, what are you doing here?"

"I have news about...what we were talking about yesterday." He eyes me up and down and I can literally feel the hairs on Rain's arms raise. He does not like this man looking at me. "Didn't know you had a little townie girl all tucked up in here. How long has this been going on?"

Rain steps between us, and I realize he's in a towel. And for a reclusive professor, he sure does look good. Not as buff as his wolf form, but he's no slouch in the muscle department. "My relationship with Paige is not your business. Now is obviously not a good time."

I'm not sure Mr. Smith is buying this, and I need him to. If he thinks that Rain and I were together in bed all night, then he won't suspect that Rain is the werewolf he shot. I need to make it clear that Rain and I are...*together*. My cheeks heat as I ponder the fib I have to weave.

"Sorry, Mr. Smith," I chime in, wrapping my arms around Rain from behind and resting my chin on his shoulder. "We were enjoying our morning together before you knocked."

Rain stiffens at my touch, but quickly relaxes, dedicating himself to the act, his fingers skimming over my knuckles in a surprisingly intimate gesture. "We were having...*breakfast*." He grins at Smith, the charm oozing from his words, masking all traces of the primal anger I know he holds buried deep within.

Smith shifts uncomfortably, his eyes darting from me to Rain, clearly taken aback by the intimacy he had inadvertently trespassed upon. He clears his throat awkwardly. "Well, my apologies for interrupting your *breakfast*," he mutters, the edges of his lips twitching with a hint of discomfort.

I can see the gears turning in his head. His gaze lingers on the lingering wetness on Rain's chest, the obvious intimacy between us. His eyes narrow for just a moment, suspicion momentarily flashes in his gaze. "I'll let you two get back to your...back to it," he says, not entirely convinced but willing to drop the matter for now.

He gives us a curt nod, backing away from the door as he takes one more look at us. With a final glance at Rain, his eyes settle on the towel around his waist, flick to me hugging him from behind, and then he turns sharply and strides down the driveway, his boots crunching against the rocks.

After ensuring that Mr. Smith is definitely out of earshot, I let go of Rain and step back. He turns to face me immediately. "That was...pretty convincing," he admits, rubbing the back of his neck awkwardly. He closes the door. "You shouldn't have embroiled yourself further in this."

"He doesn't trust you. I think he already suspects. I don't want Smith to kill you."

"Why do you care? The world would be better off without the Werewolf of Wallace Woods. You're in danger with me, Paige."

"Don't say that."

"Do you think the beast won't come looking for you at sunset? He's scented you. He believes you are his mate."

"Maybe you should stop talking about him like he's not you. You said yourself that you were in human form when you started feeling this way about me."

Rain pushes a chair out of the way, and it crashes across the room. "It's not that simple, Paige!" He paces, his movements restless and wild, like a caged animal. "The wolf...it's unpredictable, dangerous. I can control it to an extent during the day, but as night falls, it takes hold of me completely. I'm not sure I can protect you from myself," he confesses, his voice a hushed whisper filled with an undertone of terror. "You should go. Think about leaving town until I can get cleared out of here. I'll need a couple of days."

The first time he met me, yesterday in the diner, he was in human form and wanted me. Last night the beast wanted to breed me. I've dreamt about the Wolf for years.

Am I crazy to think that we are somehow linked?

I think about the way the beast's cock tasted—wild and free and...mine.

Rain turns to me, scenting the air. "You're aroused."

"Yes," I admit.

"I can smell it," he murmurs, his eyes flashing with surprise and an echo of that untamed heat, "can feel it in the air around you." His gaze rakes over me, leaving me feeling bare and vulnerable.

"And you?" I dare to ask, taking a cautious step towards him. "Are you...aroused?"

"Don't play with me, Paige. I've never felt the beast so close in daylight hours. I'm not safe for you, and you are definitely not safe for me."

I think about this, let his words roll around in my head for a minute. And then I begin to unbutton the flannel shirt of his that I threw over my naked body not very long ago.

The shirt falls away from my shoulders, pooling at my feet, until I'm standing bare before him. Rain's eyes darken, the primal force that lives within him pushing closer to the surface. He growls low in his throat, a dangerous warning that raises the hair on the back of my neck.

And then he pounces.

INSTINCT HAS ME RUNNING, even though this is what I obviously wanted. Rain tackles me to the floor. He's not in full werewolf form, but he's not exactly human either. His body is hairier, his muscles stretching bigger.

"Foolish girl," he chastises, his voice deeper now. Teeth elongating into canines, and eyes flaring amber. "Foolish, reckless girl," he repeats, but this time it's a growl, vibrating through his chest and into my skin. His weight presses me into the floor, his body a dangerous mix of man and beast.

A primal fear courses through my veins, but it's coupled with a darker, stronger desire. A desire to submit, to surrender myself completely to this being of raw, unrestrained power.

He seems to be fighting a battle within himself, battle between man and beast, a battle between desire and restraint. His fingers, now tipped with blunt claws, trace a path down my body, dragging over the sensitive skin of my breasts, my stomach, my inner thighs.

"You should run," he snarls, a low and guttural sound that rattles my bones. His fingers dig into the floor by either side of my head, claws scratching at the hardwood in a steady rhythm that echoes the pounding of my heart. His lips hover just over mine, hot breath washing over me in waves.

"But I don't want to," I admit.

He freezes at my admission, his eyes darkening further. The wolf within him takes control as he lowers his head to my neck, his canines scraping against my sensitive skin. His claws scrape downward against the floor, and a primal grunt echoes from him before he pulls away abruptly and stands, showing me once again the beast between his legs.

He's not the monster from the woods last night, but neither is he the human I spoke to moments ago. He's between worlds, and I am the anchor to both.

His chest heaves and his nostrils flare wider, taking in the scent of my fear and desire. The mixture seems to fuel the beast within him further, his eyes narrowing into dangerous slits as he gazes down at me.

"If I take you," he begins in his guttural voice. "I might hurt you. I might not be able to stop."

I raise up on my elbows. "If I run, you'll just chase me." We both know the outcome of that. Yet the gleam in his eye tells me that maybe that prey drive is what he wants to engage.

He likes it when I run.

I scrabble across the floor, but I don't get far. A low growl resonates from his chest as he launches himself at me, the primal creature within him embracing the hunt. His powerful body pins mine easily to the floor, an unyielding weight that leaves me breathless. His hot breath washes over my neck.

He flips me over and spreads my legs, nuzzling into my pussy with a hunger that has me whimpering. The rasp of his tongue is rough, a stark contrast to the softness of my most intimate folds, and I arch into the unexpected pleasure. His hands grasp my thighs, claws pricking my skin without breaking it, keeping me spread for him as he devours me.

"I warned you," his voice is a growl against my skin, vibrating with the untamed animalistic heat within him. His words are punctuated by another sweep of his tongue, which elicits a strangled cry from me.

His teeth tease against the tender flesh of my thigh, the threat of his bite sending pulses of fear and anticipation coursing through me. I can feel his control waning, his devouring kisses becoming more reckless, more dangerous.

He's making a meal out of me, and I might not live through it.

It's clear he's losing control, his body trembling with effort to not rip me apart. His claws dig deeper into my thighs, biting into my flesh as if marking his territory.

Every cell in my body knows I belong to the beast now. My limbs quake, and I start to come. Harder than I ever have before. If he doesn't kill me with his claws and teeth, I might just die from this orgasm.

It goes on and on, each wave hitting harder than the last. His tongue is relentless, a savage rhythm that drives me to the edge and then beyond. My screams echo off the walls, a primal serenade to our wildness. I come until I am breathless and light-headed, my body a writhing mass of sensation beneath his. He growls in satisfaction, the sound rumbling through the room and making me shiver in response.

His lips drift higher, tracing the curve of my hip before coming to rest on the soft swell of my abdomen. His claws retract, replaced by the tender press of his fingertips as he explores my flushed skin.

"Hush," he murmurs, his voice rough but soothing. His breath is a hot caress against my belly, his words punctuated by soft nips that send tendrils of pleasure radiating through my body. It's an alien sensation, this gentle touch after the savagery of his feast. But I find myself surrendering to it, my legs relaxing around him as he continues his exploration.

His fingers trace over my still-quivering thighs, then up to my navel. He presses a kiss there, a hot brand against my sensitized skin. And then he's exploring higher, his tongue tracing a path up my ribcage, his fingers splaying across my chest.

His breath washes over my sensitive nipple, causing it to harden immediately. He chuckles darkly before taking it into his mouth, his teeth grazing the bud in a tantalizing tease. Then he begins to suckle, each tug of his mouth pulling a moan from me, setting my skin ablaze once more.

His other hand slides around my waist, anchoring me to him as he worships my body with an adoration that takes my breath away. His lips find the hollow of my neck, and he nuzzles me as if his snout was still in wolf form.

"If you do not find a way to get away from me, little one, I will breed you until you are unconscious and then continue taking you until you wake up again."

HIS WORDS INSPIRE A reaction neither of us expect as my pussy gushes with arousal, a fresh wave of heat pooling between my thighs. His fingers tighten around my waist, his groan muffled against my flesh, the sound raw, possessive.

"Paige, you need to go. I've never gone through the change like this during the day. I don't know what I'm capable of."

His voice is strained, the edges of human dignity and control slowly fraying as the beast within him fights for dominance. But I am too drunk on his scent, his touch, his heat to consider leaving.

"I think I need this as much as you do," I tell him, honestly. "I need to feel you inside me."

"It will be a rough mating. I'm on the very edge of madness."

"I've dreamt of you. As the wolf. I have for years. Rain, your mate needs you."

His eyes flash, a predatory gleam that has me trembling. He shifts, his body coiling, muscles flexing beneath his sun-kissed skin. He's the epitome of raw power, virile masculinity. And he's all mine.

He hauls me up to my hands and knees, and I realize that though he has not changed into his beast form all the way, the cock rubbing me from behind is not human. I remember the way it tasted last night, the way it was shaped so differently from a man. I suddenly need him inside me more than air.

I wiggle my backside, hoping to entice him. My boldness earns me a possessive growl. His hands grip my hips, holding me steady as he aligns himself with my entrance. His tip is hot, burning against me, and I whimper, pushing back against him.

He rears back slightly only to plunge forward, and the force of his entrance tears a cry from my lips. The pain is like a tsunami, overwhelming and brutal. The stretch is searing, but the pleasure...oh, it's sublime. I can feel every vein, every ridge as he fills me to the brim, each thrust a testament of his primal need. His movements are savage, unyielding and fevered. My body protests the intrusion but also welcomes it, writhing and squirming beneath him.

A growl rumbles low in his chest, the sound vibrating against my back and sending shivers rippling through me. His pace quickens, every thrust a declaration of possession. I can feel him everywhere, consuming me, taking me over. The painful pleasure of it is blinding, overpowering.

"Breed," he says into my ear, his voice more beast than man. The rhythm of his thrusts increases, his command quickening my pulse. I can feel the coil within me building, building, building, threatening to snap at any moment.

"You will take my seed," he growls fiercely, the words a primal decree. His hands tighten on my hips, his thrusts becoming harder, faster. I can barely breathe, the pleasure intensifying with every second. His dominance, his power—it's all too much and yet not enough. I crave him, every element of him.

My arms are no longer strong enough to keep me on my hands and knees, so I lower my upper body to the floor, my ass still high in the air. He stills for a moment, and I feel his cock expanding inside me.

The knot.

Oh God. The knot begins to swell, his girth increasing exponentially. Panic seizes me before the all-consuming pleasure pushes it away. I shriek at the sensation, my body clenching around him and he grunts in response.

A feral growl echoes through the room as he forces himself deeper, the knot preventing him from pulling out. His movement becomes erratic, a clear sign of his impending release. The sensation overpowers me, my senses overwhelmed by this man–this beast, taking what he wants.

My pussy begins to clench around him as I come, milking him. "Come inside me," I beg, not knowing where the words come from, only that I desperately want his seed. "Breed me," I plead again, my voice low and broken.

He responds with a rough groan, teeth nipping at the nape of my neck. The sensation is sharp, sweet, and I cry out with the sheer intensity of it all.

The knot throbs and his seed spurts hot and thick inside me. His growl fills the air, raw and primal, resonating deep within my core. His rhythm falters, his body stiffening as he gives in to the pleasure. His hands on my hips tighten to the point of pain, anchoring me to him. His breathing is ragged against my ear, his heartbeat a thunderous drum against my back.

In ripples, his orgasm subsides, but he remains within me, his knot pulsating rhythmically. The hot, syrupy sensation of his seed fills me to the brim, seeping deeper into me. Our bodies are slick with sweat when he rolls us onto our sides, still connected to each other by his cock.

He wraps his limbs around me, his face in my neck. The cabin is so quiet now. I can feel his regrets as his human mind begins to wrest control of the beast.

"I can't pull out of you yet, Paige," he says quietly. "It would hurt you. I'm sorry."

"I don't want you to pull out of me," I whisper back, my voice a soft echo in the quiet cabin. He stiffens behind me for a moment before his breath exhales warmly against my skin in what might be relief. His heavy arm wraps more securely around my waist, pulling me even closer into his heat. His nose nudges into my hair and he inhales deeply, burying himself further into the scent of me, the scent of us. I can feel his chest rumble with a low growl of satisfaction at the lingering taste of our coupling.

His warm breath tickles my ear as he begins to soothe me with a low and gentle rumbling sound, like a purr. My eyes drift closed, a contentment washing over me as I slip into a sweet slumber. Everything feels as it should be.

Until I wake up.

Chapter Nine

MY EYES OPEN WIDE AS I try to remember where I am and what is happening. The blur of last night and this morning's carnal activities crash into my consciousness as I try to make sense of what is happening.

Pleasure. Pain. I'm coming. In my sleep, I am coming.

Rain is sucking on my neck and thrusting into me, his hand rolling over my clit.

"What a good girl you are," he says. "Taking me again and coming so sweetly around my cock."

I remember now that he threatened to fuck me until I passed out and fuck me again until I woke up. He wasn't joking I guess. Maybe werewolves don't know how to joke anyway.

I don't know how long I slept, if his knot subsided at all, but it is firmly in place now, locking my mate inside me. I know I will be so sore later, but it's hard to care as his cock rubs against my G-spot and sends another wave of pleasure crashing through me. His scent fills my nostrils, and I inhale deeply, committing the essence of him to memory. His hips move with a steady rhythm, his grip tight around my waist, pulling me onto him again and again. My body pulses with each thrust.

I doubt there is any room inside me for more cum, but he fills me up regardless, his wolfish growl echoing in the stillness of the cabin as he releases. The pulsing, hot sensation sends another wave of pleasure through me, a low moan escaping my lips. His grip on my waist is nearly bruising now, his knot twitching with each spurt.

Sometime later, a clock chimes. It's afternoon now.

Rain slips out of me, and the proceeds of his lovemaking trickle out from between my thighs. A low growl escapes him, possessively satisfied at the sight even as his fingers push it back to my pussy.

"That's mine," he murmurs with an intensity that sends a thrill of lust down my already quivering spine. His strong fingers are gentle now as they trace a line from the swollen lips of my sex, down to my inner thigh, smeared with his essence.

The intimacy between us changes suddenly as our brains catch up to our situation. We hardly know each other, yet here we are, his werewolf seed seeping from my womb.

"You must be hurting," he says, awkwardly. "I was very rough. I apologize."

"Please don't. Don't do this. I'm as much to blame—"

"No," he interrupts. "I'm a monster."

"Then I'm a monster fucker."

He flinches. "The primal drive...Paige, I don't know if it's possible to impregnate you. I've never changed in the daylight hours. I didn't even change all the way." He closes his eyes. "I don't know what I put into you."

"Rain—"

"You saved my life last night, and I thank you by forcing myself on you. Once while you slept. I couldn't stop myself. I have no control around you. I would love to send you into hiding to get away from me, but honestly, I don't think there is a corner of this Earth where you could hide from me."

Oh shit. There is something very wrong with me because I fucking love that. His possessiveness. His dominance. The carnal way he claims me, the raw desire in his eyes.

And I also really dig the scholar, the almost nerdy intelligence so opposite of the wolf.

"I'm not afraid of you. Maybe I should be, but I'm not. The only thing I'm afraid of right now is Mr. Smith, the hunter. I feel like he's going to figure out you're not just a scholar of folklore, but the very beast he's hunting."

Rain sighs. "I should let him kill me. That would be the safest for you."

I'm appalled. "And if I carry our child, you would leave me unprotected?"

His nostrils flare.

"Do you think Mr. Smith would just let me have your baby in peace? That he wouldn't slaughter us both—"

"Enough!" Rain shouts, the hair on his arms sprouting heavier. He takes a few long breaths and gets his feelings under control. "You're right. I can't leave you unprotected until we know you are safe from pregnancy."

I stand up on shaky legs. "We both know that you will never leave me alone until you know I am well and truly bred. And you will never leave me alone when I carry our child. We have things to discuss, but I'm hoping for a long soak if you have a bathtub. A shower at least if you don't. My car is still in a ditch on the highway, which means people are probably looking for me. My phone and clothes are in the glen where I *willingly* gave your werewolf cock a blow job last night. A hunter is trying to kill you. I haven't eaten in almost twenty-four hours. And the sun will set soon, making it hard to carry on a conversation with you because you're not a very good conversationalist when your snout gets all big."

Where my pluckiness came from, I don't know, but I barely make it to the bathroom before I collapse. What am I going to do?

• • • •

WHEN I COME OUT OF the bathroom after a good soak, I find a sandwich and a note that he will return shortly with my things. I'm rinsing my plate when he comes back with my tattered clothes and most likely toasted cellphone.

We make eye contact, and he looks away quickly. "I hope you don't mind," he says in that cultured professor voice so different from the beast, "but I arranged a tow for your car. I had to tell them that you were my girlfriend and that I picked you up. It's a small town, so I'm sure the rumor mill will work through that quickly."

I shrug. "It will surprise a lot of people, I'm sure. But mostly there will be a lot of jealous women thinking you're off the market."

He chuckles. "I'm quite a bit older than you."

That's an understatement since he hasn't actually told me how old he is, but that he lives longer than humans. Everyone in town thinks he's somewhere in his forties, so it's an age gap for sure. Also a culture gap since I'm a waitress and he's a reclusive scholar.

And I'm human and he's a werewolf.

But whatever.

"Are you very sore, Paige?"

"Deliciously sore, Rain," I answer saucily.

I can tell I befuddle him as he's trying to be reserved and stoic. "I've never...mated...in that form. I really don't know what will happen."

I sit on the couch and pat a seat next to me. "So, why do you think you changed during daylight. Your curse is from sundown to sunup."

He sits. "I've been turning it over in my mind. I just don't know. I would say it's something to do with you, but it hardly seems fair to put that on you. You told me that you have dreamed about the werewolf?"

I nod. "Yes. I've felt its...your...loneliness. That's what I wake up feeling. That and horny."

"Are they sex dreams, little one?"

I shake my head. "No. Mostly running dreams. You are chasing me, and when you catch me, I feel your loneliness."

"But you wake up..."

"Needy. Restless. Wet."

The sharp intake of his breath thrills me. "Perhaps we should not discuss that right now. I don't want to change again."

We spend another hour discussing the hunter and ways to throw him off track. We discuss all the ways he's tried to break the curse. He assures me that it was only the early days of his curse that he couldn't contain his blood lust. That the deaths he caused haunt him, but he has learned to hunt animal prey only.

After a light dinner, I turn on a lamp in the living room and we both stop cold as we realize that it's dark outside and Rain is still very human.

He hasn't changed into the beast.

Chapter Ten

"RAIN," I SAY.

He looks at his hand like it's the first time he's seeing it. The shock on his face mirrors my own. "I don't understand...it's dark, I should be...but I'm not."

We both cross the room to be closer, staring at each other in the dim light. The silence is thick with tension and unasked questions.

"Could it be...*me*?" I ask tentatively.

A loud pounding on the door startles us. He looks out the window and swears. "It's Smith again."

"This is good," I say. When he looks at me as if I were an idiot, I finish my thought. "It's nighttime. And still a full moon I think. If he suspects you are a werewolf, he won't expect your human self to answer the door.

Rain is still confused by what has transpired, but he grabs me into a quick kiss. "You are very smart." He pauses. "And very sexy wearing my shirt. You need to cover up more. If he looks at you wrong, I'm liable to change and tear his throat out."

"Let him in, I'll see if I can find a pair of your sweatpants."

I go rummage through a drawer as I hear Smith's booming voice. Oh how I'd have liked to see the look on his face when a very human Dr. Rain Stockard answered the door. Which makes me wonder why he even bothered coming here if he thought Rain would be in werewolf form and out in the woods.

Maybe Smith was checking on me. To see if he could get me to spill any of Rain's secrets. Or maybe he thought I'd be dead by werewolf by now.

I find a pair of long underwear pants, and I throw them on under Rain's flannel shirt. In the living room, I see Rain and Smith looking at a map on the desk.

"Hello again, Mr. Smith."

He says hello, but you can tell he was hoping he'd found his wolf and not just a reclusive professor who knows a lot about folklore. Maybe he'll move on someplace else now. Maybe he'll leave us alone.

I want to stand closer to Rain, give him support, but I'm afraid my presence will trigger his change again, so I take myself into the kitchen and pull out ingredients for peanut butter cookies. Stress baking seems a good use of my time. Luckily, Rain already removed the bloody towels and bandages I'd stashed in the oven earlier, or baking would not work.

Rain and Smith continue to study the map, their voices rumbling in a low drone as they discuss points of interest. The soft scrape of my wooden spoon against the mixing bowl punctuates their conversation, the comforting rhythm of stirring easing my nerves.

Smith's tone turns slightly sharp, disagreement creeping into his voice as Rain points out an area on the map. I strain my ears to try and catch their conversation. I force myself to focus on the task at hand, shaping the dough into balls.

I glance over my shoulder to find Rain's eyes on me, his attention briefly diverted from the glaring Smith. To him, I'm sure I look comically domestic in his clothes, elbow deep in cookie dough. He offers me a small smile before turning back to Smith and the map.

Their voices rise momentarily, a tinge of heated debate lacing their words. I resist the urge to drop what I'm doing and intervene. Instead, I scoop another ball of dough and set it on the baking tray.

The oven is preheated now, and as I slide the first batch of cookies into it, Smith's voice rings out above Rain's. "You spent your life studying werewolves. You telling me you really don't believe in them?"

"As I explained to you the other day, Mr. Smith, my study is of folklore. I don't believe they exist beyond the imagination. I understand your reluctance to let your life's work go, but I have nothing else to offer you. Now, I promised my girlfriend a night free of talk of my studies, and I've already gone back on my word. Maybe we can meet again in town later this week?"

Smith isn't happy that he hasn't converted Rain to his theories, but it doesn't sound like he thinks Rain is a werewolf. When he says his goodbyes, I take the cookies out of the oven and sigh in relief.

I find Rains standing at the edge of the kitchen, watching me. "I hope you don't mind me using your kitchen. I was getting antsy."

"I like you in my kitchen."

Chapter Eleven

AFTER EVERYTHING HE'S seen and done to me, it's that compliment that makes me blush. Dr. Rain Stockard likes me in his kitchen.

As humans, Rain and I would seem to have little in common, and in fact we know each other very little. It's strange to think that maybe at this very minute, I could be pregnant with his child.

Human child? Werewolf pup? How would I even know?

He comes over, and bending down, kisses the top of my head. His lips are warm and his smell is comforting. "Those cookies smell incredible."

"You can have one when they've cooled," I promise. He chuckles and gently runs his fingers over my cheek, coming back with a finger powdered with flour and a fond smile gracing his handsome face.

"I have to work tomorrow morning," I tell him.

"Do you want me to take you home now?" he asks.

I shake my head. "Unless you *want* me to go," I add. This is weird. What am I doing here?

"I don't."

We stare at each other. Awkwardly.

"Maybe we should stick close to each other," I suggest. "Until we understand more about why you didn't change into the wolf tonight."

"Perhaps that would be prudent."

I have to chuckle at his formality.

"What a strange pair we make," I say, trying to lighten the tension. Rain smiles, a genuinely warm gesture that makes his eyes sparkle.

"You're not wrong there," he agrees, his smile widening into a grin. "I'm going to shower. We'll talk more?"

I nod and gesture to the oven. "I'll finish up in here."

I'm taking the next batch of cookies out when I accidentally touch the cookie sheet. I give a quick yelp and shake out my hand, turning to the sink to put it under cold water.

Before I can even get it under there, Rain is on me. "What's wrong?" He's inspecting me for wounds.

I hold up one finger. "Just a little burn. I'm fine."

His arms are in full-werewolf hair mode, and he's sporting some pretty spectacular sideburns.

"Rain, I'm fine. I promise."

He growls and pulls my hand under cold water while the rest of my body is sheltered in his half-changed form. I can't help but lean into the solid mass of him behind me. And it seems he can't help but sniff my neck.

When my poor finger is good and numb, he wraps my hand in a towel and pats it dry. His body is changing again, the fur receding.

"You test my control," he finally says.

"Maybe. But I think I'm the reason you're not howling at the moon right now though, too."

He nods. "In all my research to break my curse, I've never come across anything about a plucky waitress being the key."

I laugh. "Well, you might have to update your resources then." A smile flits across my face as I reach up to trace the last of the disappearing fur from his cheek. His skin is warm and slightly rough beneath my fingers. "Do you still think I should be afraid of you?" I ask.

"It's becoming clear to me that I would rather die than hurt you, Paige. But when I change I don't have control of the beast."

"That's not true. You told me that you haven't hunted humans since you first turned. You didn't hurt me in your beast form in the forest last night, and you didn't hurt me this morning when you were half changed either."

"How can you say that?" He pulls the collar of my shirt to reveal all the bites he left on my skin. "And who knows what I've done to you internally? You are too small to take my cock." His cheeks pinken. "Especially the knot."

"And yet, I *did* take your cock. And I *did* take your knot. And I came over and over. I happen to like the marks you left all over me."

"And if you die giving birth to a monster, will you like that as well?"

My blood runs cold. "Do not talk about our child that way," I grind out, more angry than I think I've ever been in my entire life. I don't even know where the feeling came from.

We're both breathing hard and the tension in the air is thick. He stares at me, bewildered, visibly shaken by the intensity in my voice.

"I didn't mean—" he starts, but I cut him off.

"No," I say, my voice as cold as the water that had numbed my finger earlier.

"Don't say anything else until you listen and really hear me. If I am pregnant then it's because I am meant to be. If I have changed your curse, if I have somehow bent the laws of physics to take your giant cock inside my body and didn't get torn in half from it, then I am damn well sure that if anyone is supposed to carry your child, it's me. And you can tell me over and over how dangerous you are, but you were ready to tear the roof off this house when I got a burn the size of a pencil eraser on my finger. You are not dangerous to *me*."

He blinks at me in surprise, his handsome face frozen in a mask of shock that slowly recedes into contrition. "I apologize," he intones, his voice so full of regret it threatens to undo me right then and there. "I may be a werewolf, but you are a force of nature, Paige."

The corner of my mouth lifts in a small smile. "You're just now figuring that out?"

It seems like the tension has been broken. Things are calm. And then we're closing the distance, and I'm in his arms, his mouth capturing mine, his hands pulling apart the shirt I'm wearing as buttons skitter across the kitchen.

He's primal for sure, but still completely human. At least for now. His hands are sliding down my back, up my sides, palming my breasts. I'm tugging him closer. I can't get close enough.

He pauses, rimming a circle around my nipple with his finger. "It's so wrong of me, but I can't wait to see these filled up and milky." He squeezes my breast like he's half expecting it to already be full.

"Is this milky boob fetish a Professor Stockard kink or a Wolf of Wallace Woods kink?" I tease.

He growls against my neck, a low rumble that sends a shiver through me. "Both." He weighs my breasts in his hands. "They will be impossibly heavy, even more beautiful than they already are." His voice is a throaty growl, full of male satisfaction and a smoky desire. "Sweet milk for the baby. For me."

He draws on a nipple but makes eye contact with me. We're both imagining him drinking from my milky tits, and when did that become a thing I might like? God the thought is so primal, so raw, it stirs something inside me that I can hardly comprehend. I blush, but his eyes hold mine with a hunger that makes me arch and whimper softly. His hands are firm on my body as he pulls me against him, a silent promise of what is to come.

• • • •

HE CARRIES ME TO THE bedroom, his footsteps heavy and steady on the wooden floorboards, the moonlight filtering through the window casts a silver glow on everything. He places me gently onto the bed, his gaze never leaving mine. I watch as he strips his own clothes off, his body bathed in the ephemeral light of the moon, every muscle defined, his skin glowing. He moves without hesitation, a predator closing in on its prey, yet there's an intimacy in his eyes that tugs at my heart.

He crawls onto the bed, the mattress dipping under his weight, and cages me in with his strong arms. His hands roam my body again, tracing the curves and valleys with a reverence that makes me feel like a work of art being studied. One hand slides down my belly, his fingers dancing over my stomach in a gentle caress that sparks a warmth inside me. His other hand lifts my chin, forcing me to look at him.

His eyes are a storm, swirling with emotions too complex to name as his thumb gently traces the contours of my lips. He bends down, capturing my mouth in a languid kiss that makes me sigh darkly. He takes the opportunity to deepen the kiss, his tongue gently exploring, tasting, claiming. The world beyond our little bubble ceases to exist. There's only him and me, the heat between us, and the primal instinct that draws us closer, to be as close as we can.

To mate.

He pulls back ever so slightly, his breath mingling with mine, his forehead resting against mine. His eyes are hooded with intensity, his pupils dilated.

"Mine," he rasps, voice thick with raw possessiveness and need. "I want to make love to you, Paige. Will you allow me to be your lover? As a man?"

"I'm more afraid of you in human form than I am of your beast." I close my eyes. "You're making my heart feel so tender."

"I will protect your tender heart with everything I have," he whispers into my ear, his warm breath sending goosebumps skittering across my skin.

Why does this feel so right? How can it? We hardly know each other.

His hand lifts from my belly to rest on my heart, fingers splayed wide, feeling the throb of my pulse beneath his touch. He watches me intensely as though he can see every emotion and thought churning inside me. The moonlight filters in from the window, painting his face in soft hues of silver and blue. I reach out to trace the shape of his cheekbone, feeling the rough stubble beneath my fingers.

"I do want you to be my lover. In any form that you come in," I say, simply.

"You're very special, Paige. I'm worried that all I can offer you is half a life. A life lived in shadows. But even as my scholarly pursuits have long ruled out this kind of connection, I admit that every cell in my body tells me that you are my mate." He gazes at me with a concentration that takes my breath away, his thumb circling over the steady beat of my pulse. "I've walked alone a long time, but you are still so young."

"I *am* young. And I read a lot, but I'm not educated like you are. What if I'm not enough for *you*?" I whisper, my eyes meeting his in the soft moonlight.

His thumb pauses against my pulse, and for a moment, he is silent. "If we can accept a world with werewolves, we should be able to accept a world of fated mates, little one. You stir my blood and soothe it at the same time. If I had a chance to change the night I was cursed, but it meant never meeting you, I wouldn't do it. I couldn't, not even if I know you're better off not knowing me."

His words land heavily in the silence of the room and a soft sigh escapes my lips as I instinctively press closer into his embrace. The moonlight seems to hold its breath, the room descending into a hushed stillness.

And then he slides inside me, the hardness of him familiar. The shape as it was when he was in wolf form. The rest of him is all human. But his cock is not. "How?"

He chuckles. "All the better to breed you with."

ONE YEAR LATER

The baby is awake. Again.

I roll over, but Rain's hand stills me. "I'll get him, little one. Rest here, I'll bring him to you after he's changed."

Rain slips from our bed, and I watch through half-lidded eyes as he disappears into the nursery, and a few moments later, the soft coos and gurgles of our son reach my ears. My weariness subsides a little at the sound, replaced by a warmth that radiates from my heart and seeps into every corner of my body.

The door creaks open, and Rain reappears with our squirming bundle of joy cradled in his strong arms. The moonlight filters through the window, casting a halo around his tousled hair and painting our son's cherub-like cheeks with a soft glow. The sight of them, my boys, my family, stirs something deep within me, and I can't help the tender smile that tugs at my lips.

Our babe shows no signs of canine anything. Though Rain remains with a foot in both worlds.

Rain is gentle as he hands the baby to me. Our son's eyes, so like his father's, look up at me as I cradle him to my chest. He latches on to feed, and I let out a soft sigh of contentment. Rain settles down beside us, his hand coming to rest on our son's fuzzy head, stroking gently in a soothing rhythm.

As the baby suckles, Rain's fingertips trace a path from our son's forehead to his tiny nose and finally his rosy cheeks, each touch filled with unspoken love and adoration. Warmth floods my body as I take in the sight, the quiet intimacy of this moment binding us together as nothing else could.

"Never thought I would have this," Rain says, his voice barely more than a whisper. His gaze never leaves our son, his hand continuing its loving caress. He swallows before he continues. "This...peace, this love. It's more than I ever hoped for. Even before the curse, I thought I was destined to be a lifelong bachelor. I was a perfect ass and deserved to be punished. I was terrible to women. And I never wanted a commitment. Never wanted children. I'd have died a lonely old man if the witch hadn't cursed me. Then I thought I'd maybe never die. Just be half man half monster haunting the Earth forever."

The silence stretches between us as I just watch him, my heart swelling with emotion. "Well, you're not alone anymore."

Things are still difficult, of course. Rain doesn't change into the wolf every sunset anymore, but the beast is always just below the surface for him. Sometimes we don't know what sets off his change.

Sometimes, I *do* know what sets off his change, though. And I do it on purpose. Rain's beast has a strong prey drive. All I have to do is run to engage it.

The chase is always exhilarating, filled with a thrill that I have yet to grow tired of. I run. He chases. There is always that moment of fear, of uncertainty when I feel his hot breath on my heels, his low growl echoing through the forest.

When he catches me, the powerful, dominating wolf takes over, pressing me into the soft earth with his bulk. His teeth graze my shoulder in a warning. I usually fight him. It's instinct, after all. But I'm no match for his strength. His claws lightly scratch my sides, a mere hint of the power he possesses. He's careful with me, always careful. The rawness of his nature is tempered by the love he holds for me.

My biggest fear remains to be the hunter. Mr. Smith. He's still out there somewhere. Still hunting for my husband or beasts like him.

We've moved to an even smaller town in the mountains. The air here is crisp and clear, filled with the scent of pine and the distant sound of a rushing river. Our home is a cozy place, nestled deep within the wilderness, far from the prying eyes of man.

The baby finishes his meal, and Rain brings him back to his crib. I'm feeling...needy. Rain returns to our room, his gaze catching mine. His eyes smolder with the same heat I feel in my own. He pads across the room toward me, his grace reminding me of the wolf within him as he gets into bed. His hands reach out for me and pull me close. I sink into him, wrapping my arms around him, my skin tingling under his touch. His scent envelops me, earth and musk, a heady combination that awakens an insatiable need.

"Rain," I murmur into his neck, as he rolls me onto my back, hovering over me. "I need you."

The coarse hair of his arm thickens. The low rumble in his chest evolves into something deeper, grittier. His fingers flex against my hips, the nails lengthening into claws. I hold him tighter, my heart fluttering in anticipation.

He bends down to flick his tongue on one of my nipples. His mouth is hot, and I gasp as he gently pulls on me with his lips, sending lances of pleasure straight to my core. His fingers dig into my flesh, each touch sparking a fevered reaction deep within me. Our eyes meet, and I see the wildness there.

His hands ruck up my nightgown, and he tests my readiness. "So wet, Mrs. Stockard." His voice is gravelly, the beast within him straining against the veneer of his humanity.

Kissing me deeply, he slowly drinks in my sighs as he slides inside me, thick and hot, while he attacks my breast again. My milk lets down, and he drinks until I'm left panting, every nerve in my body alight with his touch. He sets a brutal pace, each thrust coaxing another moan from my lips, and I wrap my legs around him to pull him deeper.

My hands grip his back, nails scraping over skin. His growl vibrates against my chest, his rhythm begins to falter, his strokes growing more erratic as we get closer to the edge. His grunts punctuate the silence of our room, mixing with the soft sound of our bodies meeting. I lose myself in him, my world narrowing to us, to this moment.

"I'm going to fill you with another babe, wife."

His words send a thrill through me, igniting the fire in my belly. He buries his face in the crook of my neck as he continues to thrust into me. His pace is relentless, stirring me closer and closer to the edge. I hold onto him as if my life depends on it, the waves of pleasure beginning to crash against the walls of my being. I let out a whimper, the raw, primal sound ripped from deep within me, echoing off the wooden beams above us.

Suddenly, he growls against my skin, a low, feral sound that vibrates through me as he drives into me with primal force. "Are you ready for my knot, little one. Is your pussy ready to take all of me?" His words are delivered in a carnal growl, a predatory promise I welcome with an urgent nod.

Within moments, I feel him swell inside me, an unyielding bulge that stretches me to my limits and guides us both over the precipice of pleasure. Gasping, kicking, reeling beneath the force of our shared climax, my breasts are leaking between us. I feel him shudder and draw in a ragged breath above me. He grinds into me, each pulse filling me further until we're both spent and panting, the room filled with the scent of raw, primal sex.

He collapses onto me, his weight an anchor holding me to the earth as my body continues to quiver, the aftershocks of our pleasure still rippling through me. His breath is hot and ragged against my neck, the rhythm matching the steady thud of my own heart. Our bodies are slick with sweat and milk, tangled together in the aftermath of our carnal dance.

And of course, we're stuck together, his cum trapped inside me by the swell of him that refuses to wane. His knot ensures there is nowhere for it to go, that his seed will stay where he wants it—inside me. His roughened hands are gentle as they stroke my sides, tracing patterns on my sweat-slick skin. My fingers play idly with the hairs at the nape of his neck, a soothing rhythm that lulls us both into a blissful post-coital haze. His lips tenderly press against my throat, quiet whispers of affection barely audible above our breathing.

As a girl, I felt bad for Belle when she went through all that and her beast turned into a prince. I'm lucky to live in both worlds— to have my beast, and keep him too.

MEET ALISON, A COLLEGE student who's been living two lives. By day, she's a shy wallflower, but in her private moments alone with her e-reader, she indulges in her secret passion for monster romance, dreaming of a world where she too could be swept away by creatures of her deepest fantasies.

But when Alison wakes up in the realm of El, it's not just her dream coming true—it's a nightmare. Her guide in the twisted realm, the Dark Prince Mavius, wants to populate his kingdom by breeding her to the monsters of El. She'll be initiated by each one and may the best sperm win.

She agrees to submit to Mavius and his monsters, thinking it's just an erotic dream. And in her dreams, Alison wants to be taken roughly and filled with the seed of creatures not of her world. But despite his wicked game, Alison can't help the desire Mavius ignites within her even as he watches her being bred by others.

Mavius may be the most dangerous monster of all. And it's his darkness that calls to her the most.

Author Confession: I love monster romance, but a lot of the heroes seem pretty beta lately. I like a monster who knows he's a damn monster. Which is to say there are no alphamallows inside this story. Here there be monsters. And a bit of dubious consent, but not really. And if breeding kink is your jam, buckle up, this is your seed-filled jam for sure. Look for an orc, a minotaur, a werewolf...and a happy ending because it's still romance after all.

Chapter One

I'M NESTLED IN THE small bed of my dorm room, the dim glow of my e-reader casting shadows on the walls as I turn the digital pages of my latest download—monster romance novel.

God, how I wish the creatures in the books were real. I don't know how I first found out about the genre, but I was hooked instantly, like I'd been waiting for them my whole life. I belong in that world. The one with beasts and monsters. Creatures that take what they want and protect what is theirs.

They're powerful, barbaric, raw. Nothing like the guys I've ever been around. Maybe it's the idea of being with someone who lives by their primal desires. Or maybe it's the forbidden nature of it, the thrill of being with a creature that society deems as monstrous. Whatever it is, I can't help but feel a deep yearning for that kind of passion and intensity in my own life.

The more taboo the books are, the more I seem to like them. Something in me is darker than the girls around me, I think. In books, I can free that part. Because in reality, I'm just a quiet, unremarkable girl, lost in the sea of faces on campus, living in a world of boring, safe nothingness.

Every day, the walls of my dorm room feel like they're closing in on me. It's the same bland life every day, with nothing but the flicker of my eReader for company. I've always been a bit of a wallflower, but coming to this all-girls university has only amplified the feeling of being on the fringes of everything. Worse, it's the ridiculous kind of school where we have to wear uniforms and go to services twice a week like we're still in prep school or something.

I watch from the sidelines as cliques of girls my age whisper and giggle, going out to parties and having fun. They don't invite me. I don't even think they *see* me.

And when we do have co-ed activities with the men's college, I can't help but feel like a fish out of water. I don't know how to interact with the guys, how to flirt, or even how to dress. It's like I'm stuck in a perpetual state of awkwardness.

I don't belong here. I've never belonged anywhere. There's something about me that just doesn't fit. Like I was meant for a different planet or realm or something.

My eyelids grow heavy, but I don't want to sleep. Not yet. This book is too good. It's by far the dirtiest book I've ever read.

I'm a good girl. I've always been a good girl. I'm not supposed to be reading these dirty books, letting them fill my head with dirty thoughts and dirty desires. I shouldn't let my fantasies run away with me.

But I can't help it.

I want to be dominated. Owned. Claimed.

And I find I want to be a little bit scared.

The book I'm reading is like crack. My breathing is shallow, my heart beating fast as I read. With one hand, I reach between my thighs, cupping my sex through my panties. The thought of being taken, lost in the throes of passionate fantasy, is making me dripping wet. I touch my clit. My climax hits me hard.

But even though I came, I feel so empty inside.

I put my reader on the nightstand. I need to get some sleep. Tomorrow is another boring day.

• • • •

I'M IN A GRAVEYARD unlike any I've ever seen before. It's beautiful, otherworldly, and filled with vibrant, alien flowers. An ethereal moonlight dances across the landscape. The air is rich with the scent of life and magic, intoxicating me with its enchanting aroma. I am awestruck by the beauty and strangeness of this place, feeling both thrilled and overwhelmed.

"Welcome to El," a deep voice purrs behind me, causing my breath to catch in my throat. I whirl around to find a tall, dark figure emerging from the shadows. His eyes are obsidian, burning with an intensity that holds me captive. He extends a hand towards me, his fingers tipped with sharp, black claws. "I am the Dark Prince Mavius."

I can't tear my eyes away from those claws as he takes my hand and kisses it.

"Wh-why am I here? How did I get here?" I stammer, my pulse quickening. I look around and see that I am surrounded by a myriad of strange, twisted tombs and crypts. A macabre array of mausoleums, spires, and sepulchers stretch out in all directions.

Instead of answering me, the dark prince takes my hand and leads me further into the graveyard. We walk past strange headstones inscribed with arcane symbols and rows of eerie marble statues that seem to watch us as we pass by.

As eerie as the graveyard is, it's beautiful in a dark, mysterious way. There is a strange, wild energy in the air.

Prince Mavius stops in front of a large crypt adorned with intricate carvings of dragons and serpents. The door is made of pure black obsidian, and as he places his hand on it, it glows with an eerie green light.

"My dear Alison," he says, a wicked grin spreading across his face as he steps closer to me. "I have brought you here because I have need of your...unique abilities." His gaze travels up and down my body, igniting a fire within me that I struggle to suppress.

"Unique abilities? What do you mean?" I ask, my curiosity piqued despite the danger I can sense radiating from him. Nobody in my real life thinks I'm unique in any way. Least of all me.

"Your vivid imagination, your longing for adventure...I've enjoyed watching your fevered dreams. I steal into them often. You're a hot little trollop, aren't you?"

I gasp. What to unpack first? That he steals into my dreams? Or that he called me a trollop?

"You are the perfect candidate to help me populate my kingdom with offspring unlike any this realm has ever seen," he explains, his voice like velvet as it caresses my ears.

I take a step back, uncertainty and fear warring within me. "I don't understand. How am I supposed to help you populate your kingdom?"

"By surrendering yourself to the creatures of El and allowing them to breed with you," he replies, his eyes never leaving mine. "I know what you want, Alison. I know you want to be filled with the seed of a monster. I know you want to submit and be marked roughly."

Holy shit. "You don't know anything about me."

"Don't I? I've seen your dreams. I've watched you in your sad little room. Many times, little one."

He's a stalker. He's a nightmare come to life.

He's everything I dream of.

Which means there is something very wrong with me.

"The smell of your fear is almost as intoxicating as the smell of your innocence." His eyes get even blacker. "I want to give you your every fantasy. El was made for naughty human girls like you."

I shake my head, looking around this graveyard for the way out. How did I even get here? "I want to go home."

"Do you?" He puts an arm around me and waves his hand at a pool of water. The water becomes a movie, showing me a huge naked monster looking at…is that me? The creature's cock, dark and ominous, twitches with lust as it steps forward. It's so big. Huge. I've never seen anything like it. It's at least ten inches long, thick and veiny with a bulbous head covered in ridges that look almost like scales.

"You mean you don't want that monster cock parting your pussy lips, sliding into you? Are you sure? It's so big and rough, almost too big for your innocent little cunt. It will stretch you wide, fill you to the brim."

I try to shrug out of his one-armed embrace, but he digs his claws in, just a little, so I stop moving. Movie me is moaning and whimpering as she spreads her legs and arches her back as the monster saws in and out of her. Then he stops moving, holding utterly still.

"Do you know what he's doing, Alison?" I shake my head. "He's holding her down because his cock is starting to swell, it's throbbing and pulsing as it prepares to breed her. It's going to spurt hot, sticky seed inside her, fill her up."

Then the picture vanishes, and it's just a pool of water again. I almost collapse.

"I can smell your desire, Alison. You can't hide it from me."

Wait. This is a dream. It must be. Things start to click, making more sense. I fell asleep reading one of my books.

Of course this is a dream.

Okay, okay. I take a closer look at this Dark Prince Mavius and breathe a sigh of relief. I'm not attracted to him because I'm damaged. I'm attracted to him because I'm *dreaming*.

"So you're saying I would get to live out my wildest fantasies, here in El?" I ask, my heart pounding with the excitement of the possibility. It's only a dream, but what an incredible opportunity to explore my deepest, darkest desires.

"Indeed," the prince confirms, a wolfish smile gracing his lips. "But only if you are willing to submit yourself completely to me and the creatures of this realm."

I swallow hard, the thought both thrilling and terrifying. But this is a dream. I glance around at the beauty and the macabre of El, and part of me craves the adventure that awaits. A spark ignites within me, urging me to accept his proposal and see where this journey leads.

"All right," I whisper, my voice barely audible. "I'll do it."

"Excellent," he purrs, his eyes darkening with satisfaction.

I stare at him, my body trembling with desire and uncertainty. His dark eyes hold a magnetic pull that I can't seem to resist.

"How does this work, exactly?"

"You will lay with several creatures, over and over, until you are successfully bred."

"Creatures?" I ask, my voice barely above a whisper as I imagine the mythological beings I've only read about in my novels.

"Each creature is unique, each one offering you unimaginable pleasure," he explains. "And each one will be single-mindedly trying to fuck a baby into you."

This is quite possibly the best dream ever.

"However," the prince adds, his tone serious, "there are conditions you must adhere to. You must submit to me and every monster completely. You cannot say no to *any* demand. And if any creature fails to make you orgasm, I will release you back to your world."

"But this is just a dream."

"If you say so."

"So, if I say no, I wake up?"

"If you say no, you can never return to El."

I hope my alarm doesn't wake me up before the good stuff.

"I agree to your conditions."

"Excellent," he purrs, his eyes darkening with satisfaction. "We are bound."

A chill runs through me at his vow, the kind that makes me question if this is really happening. Can it be true? No, it must be a dream. Just a very vivid one.

Because if it's not a dream, then I just promised a dark prince of an alternate reality that no matter what he asks of me, I am not allowed to say no. That I am completely under his power.

Probably, I'm fine. Probably.

But what if he forces me to do...I don't know what. I mean if this isn't a dream, then I'm going to lose my virginity to a mythological monster and have sex with many more until I am pregnant. I have a calc test in the morning. I eat instant ramen for most meals. I am not ready to be pregnant.

And what if they hurt me?

"Be at ease, Alison," the prince murmurs as he touches my trembling hand. "I promise to protect you and guide you through your journey in El." His eyes hold my gaze, offering reassurance and something else. I just don't know what. "Any pain you feel will result in immediate and equal pleasure," he says, his voice deep and velvety. "You must trust me, for we are bound by our agreement."

A small nod is all I can manage, my heart pounding as I try to process the enormity of the situation. I take a deep breath, focusing on his presence and the warmth of his hand enveloping mine.

"Your first act of submission," he continues, "is to remove your nightclothes and let me inspect all your naughty, naughty bits."

My cheeks flame with embarrassment and vulnerability, but I don't protest; after all, I agreed to submit to him completely. Slowly, I reach for the hem of my sleep t-shirt, pulling it upward as the cool air of the graveyard brushes against my skin. He indicates that my panties must go, so I push them down and step out.

No one has ever seen me naked before, and I'm completely exposed.

"Exquisite," he breathes, taking a step back to fully appreciate my body. He inhales deeply, a predatory smile playing at his lips. "You are fertile."

I want to cover up. He seems to find pleasure in my discomfort. At my vulnerability.

"Remember, Alison," he says softly, circling around me like a predator stalking its prey. "For the rest of your time in El, you are my toy." The words send a shudder through me, igniting a mix of emotions within. Is this really what I want?

I inhale deeply and meet his eyes, steeling myself for the unknown. "Yes, Dark Prince Mavius," I say, my voice filled with determination. "I am your toy."

"Good," he says, a wicked grin spreading across his face. "I've seen you reach your peak many times, so I will know if you try to fake an orgasm."

I blink my surprise. "How have you—"

He grabs a handful of my hair and yanks it abruptly, that sharp pain sending tingles directly to my clit. "I told you, I've watched you." he seethes. "I've watched you in your room and I've watched you in your dreams. I perhaps know you better than you know yourself."

As I stand there, naked and trembling, I feel my limits being tested already and we haven't even begun.

Chapter Two

PRINCE MAVIUS LEADS me out of the graveyard and into the woods, the moonlight casting shadows through the thick canopy of leaves above us. The forest seems ancient and alive with secrets, its dark embrace both soothing and menacing. My bare feet sink into the soft moss, and I shiver as a cool breeze rustles the leaves, the scent of damp earth filling my nostrils. Occasionally, we pass stone remnants of buildings that no longer exist.

I'm now dressed in a long white nightgown like an innocent maiden lost in a fairy tale. The delicate fabric clings to my body, emphasizing every curve, as if designed for this very moment—to be sacrificed to a creature of the night.

"Alison," Mavius says, his voice low and seductive, "you must remember that your best chance of not getting hurt is to allow the creatures to do whatever they want to you, however they want, and for as long as they want." His eyes are serious, but there's a hint of a smile playing at the corner of his lips. "They're aware that humans are fragile creatures, and they will do their best not to damage you. But their primal natures are strong and hard to overcome."

I nod, trying to still the tremble in my limbs. My heart races with both fear and anticipation as he continues.

"Be submissive, Alison. The more yielding you are, the easier it will be for you. Especially with the orc," he says, his gaze locked on mine. "His appearance can be...intimidating. Especially his cock. And his balls..." Mavius pauses, holding his hands apart to demonstrate, "His balls are the size of your human softballs. You should expect his ejaculation to be powerful and last a long time."

I swallow hard, the image he paints both terrifying and arousing. It's difficult to imagine such a creature, let alone submit to him utterly. The thought sends a shudder through my body, igniting a primal heat deep within me. I am to be bred by these creatures, and the orc first among them. As the forest surrounds us, I steel myself for what is to come, surrendering to the desires that Mavius has awakened in me.

"One more thing. The orc likes a chase," he says. "Run," Mavius commands, his whip cracking through the air like a gunshot.

The sound and his sudden and out-of-place command startle me. I don't take the time to think. I just start running, my body smarter than my head has been since I arrived, knowing that danger is bad and I should flee. I should have from the moment I got here.

Heart pounding, I sprint into the depths of the forest, branches whipping at my face as my long white nightgown billows around me. My breath comes in ragged gasps, the thrill of the hunt mingling with my fear of the unknown. The shadows cast by ancient trees and thick foliage loom menacingly around me.

As I run, my thoughts race back to Mavius's words. Be submissive. Yield. The more I give in to these creatures, the safer I will be.

Suddenly, strong arms wrap around me from behind, bringing me crashing down onto a bed of cool, damp moss. My pulse quickens as I find myself pinned beneath the hulking form of the orc.

"Female," he growls, his voice deep and guttural, his large, protruding tusks jut out from his lower jaw. He towers over me, green skin glistening with sweat, his brutish muscular frame rippling with power. His eyes burn red with a feral energy that both terrifies and excites me.

He's not in any way as attractive as some of the orcs on my book covers. More monster than man.

"Please," I whisper, my voice trembling, "don't hurt me."

He snarls in response, tearing my gown apart with one swift motion. The cold air kisses my exposed flesh, making me shiver with vulnerability.

"Orc eat human."

Oh, fuck. He's going to kill me? I try to roll out of his grasp, but he's so strong. There's nothing I can do but go limp and accept my fate.

I don't want to die.

As the orc lowers his head, I brace myself for a savage attack.

He's savage, but not what I expected.

His long, black tongue laps at my pussy, the sensation crude and intense. My initial shock gives way to arousal, as if some primal part of me yearns for this. I struggle to reconcile my innocence with the intensity of the experience, my sense of self slipping away like sand through my fingers.

This is all that matters now.

"God," I moan, the pleasure building inside me as his tongue works its magic, my mind a haze of ecstasy and confusion.

"More," he demands, his voice rough with hunger. "Submit, female."

I try to cling to the remnants of reality, but it's like trying to hold onto a fading dream. The raw desire coursing through me is undeniable, and I find myself submitting to the orc's primal needs, spreading my legs wider.

His eyes gleam with wicked triumph, and he redoubles his efforts. The sensations are nearly unbearable—so intense that I feel as though I'm being torn apart and remade in the throes of pleasure. And yet, I crave more.

He alternates between licking me and fucking me with his tongue. His very long, slender tongue.

"Harder," I beg, surprising even myself with the urgency in my voice. The orc, eager to comply, buries his face deeper between my legs, his green tongue working relentlessly within me. How I am not getting gored by tusks, I don't know.

Then his long, thin tongue touches something deep inside me and I gush, something I've never done before. The sounds of him rooting around my sloppy pussy are obscene but now I can't stop coming.

With each shattering roll of my orgasm, I embrace the darkness within, allowing it to mingle with the orc's primal energy.

"Female," he growls, his voice thick with satisfaction. "You belong to me now."

And at that moment, as I lie trembling beneath him, covered in sweat and desire, I know the truth: that I do, indeed, belong to him. That this wild, untamed realm of monsters and magic has claimed me already, body and soul.

"Yours, orc," I whisper, my voice filled with surrender. "I am yours."

The orc finally releases me, and I relax on the soft moss beneath us, my body still trembling from the onslaught of pleasure. He rises to his full height, towering over me like a dark, menacing statue. My breath catches as he removes his loincloth, revealing what lies hidden beneath.

Even though Mavius had tried to prepare me for this moment, I am rendered speechless by the sight of him. The orc's cock is unlike anything I have ever seen–thick, ridged over the entire length, and pulsing with raw, unbridled power. A dollop of milky white liquid glistens at the tip, hinting at the torrent that awaits me.

"Female," he growls, his voice low and guttural. "You will bear my mark."

With deliberate, measured movements, the creature rubs his monstrous cock all over my body, smearing his precum on my skin like he's buttering his toast. I'm covered in it. I shudder beneath him, feeling both humiliated and aroused by my submission to him.

"Please," I whimper, uncertain of what I am even asking for. But the orc understands, and he positions the head of his cock on top of my clit.

"Be ready, female," he warns and then begins rubbing his engorged head against my sensitive nub. My inner walls clench, yearning for the fullness that only this orc can provide.

This is not the way I planned to lose my virginity, but it's what I'd always secretly hoped for.

"Y-yes," I pant, my voice raw and desperate. "I want it... Please... Fill me."

With an animalistic growl, he slowly begins to push his massive cock inside me. The stretch is painful, but there's a perverse satisfaction in knowing I am taking something so enormous, so utterly not human. As he continues to thrust deeper, I feel as though I am being split apart—and yet, I crave more. The ridges bump along my inner walls.

"More," I beg, my voice hoarse with need. "Please... I want all of you."

"Good female," he rumbles approvingly, and with a final, powerful thrust, he buries himself to the hilt within me.

I cry out.

As my body adjusts to his size, my fear and trepidation begin to fade, replaced by a growing sense of confidence and desire. I find myself matching his rhythm, meeting each of his brutal thrusts with one of my own. Together, we become a force of nature, our bodies colliding with primal ferocity.

"More," I moan, my inhibitions crumbling like the walls of a castle under siege.

"Hush, female," he grunts, increasing the intensity of his thrusts until my vision blurs from the sheer force of our coupling.

As his cock slams into me with relentless abandon, I relinquish control, letting the storm sweep me away. I scream as a new climax tears through me like a hurricane, leaving nothing but shivering wreckage in its wake.

"Take it, female," he growls, his voice a rough command that sends a shiver down my spine. "Take my seed and bear my offspring."

His words ignite a deep yearning that I can no longer deny. My body quivers with anticipation as I feel the slow, deliberate pulsing of his cock inside me, signaling the beginning of his long, drawn-out release.

The monster lets out a guttural roar, and I can feel his cock twitching and throbbing as he floods me with his essence. The sensation is overwhelming, pleasure mingling with an odd sense of fulfillment.

"More," I whimper, my nails digging into the moss beneath me as I arch my back, desperate for every last drop of him. "Please, don't stop."

He grunts, his massive hands gripping my hips tightly as he continues to pump his seed into me.

My body is racked with pleasure as each spurt of his hot seed fills me to the brim, threatening to spill over. The orc finishes with a last spurt, and as he releases me, I collapse onto the bed of moss, my body trembling and drenched in sweat, orc seed, and my own arousal. I lie there, panting, unable to comprehend what has just happened.

My eyes close, and I am more relaxed than I've ever been. I no longer feel the orc near me. He must have gone. There was no tenderness between us, but I am surprised that I feel bereft. All he wanted was my pussy. A vessel to hold his cum.

That is what I am here. I am a whore to be bred. They will use me and forget about me.

I raise up to my elbows and see the Dark Prince Mavius. He begins a slow clap, mocking me, I think.

"Very impressive, Alison," Mavius purrs, his eyes glinting with satisfaction. "You have proven yourself to be quite the eager orc slut."

His words should sting, but instead, they fuel my newfound hunger for the creatures of this world.

"Yes, Your Majesty. I guess I am."

"You were made for this, Alison. You were born to bear the children of monsters."

THE FOREST AROUND ME stutters, like it is moving but I am not. And then I find myself in a new setting.

As I step into the entrance of the labyrinth, the damp stone walls close in around me, and my heart races with a mixture of excitement and fear. Once again, I'm wearing a virginal white nightgown, like I did in the forest.

I wonder if I will ever see the orc again. I relive the feeling of his rough, primal fucking and his thick, ridged cock that brought me so much pleasure. The way he absolutely flooded me. The way he just left me when he was through.

I know I am not here to have relationships with these monsters, not like my romance novels, but I have probably already formed an ill-advised attachment to the orc.

And Mavius, but I can't think about that right now. Instinctively, I know that Mavius is the most dangerous monster of all.

The air is thick and heavy in the labyrinth, a corporeal cloud of lust that clings to my skin. I venture further into the labyrinth, the darkness swallowing me whole. As I turn each corner and navigate through the twists and turns of the maze, the weight of an otherworldly presence bears down on me. My breaths become shallow and quick, my body craving the encounter that awaits as much as it fears it.

There is a sudden clattering, an echo. The ground shakes. A huffing, snorting sound that raises the hair on my neck. The sound echoes through the corridors, sending a jolt of anticipation through my core. My pulse quickens.

The heavy breathing and footsteps grow louder, intensifying my fear. And my anticipation. The air in the labyrinth grows thicker. Heavier. A fog of pheromones and musk.

And then a large shadow nearly fills the wide corridor in front of me. I try to swallow my fear but choke on it as the mass moves toward me. I stop and my next monster turns the corner into my direct line of vision.

Fight or flight passes me right by as I choose *freeze*. I stand perfectly still, barely breathing, barely blinking.

A minotaur. Half man. Half bull.

Massive and heavily muscled. He looks to be twice my size as he gets closer.

He's disconcerting. A mix of features that should not go together. The face of a bull with human expression. A head topped with horns. Big ones.

The minotaur stands upright like a man, well, if a man had horns, but he has fur-covered legs leading to his cloven hooves.

A musky scent wafts from his fur and skin, and immediately my pussy begins to throb. He is the monster that has haunted some of my most fevered dreams.

And he is beautiful.

He stops in front of me. I stare into his eyes, and he snorts, lowering his head so we are face to face. My knees quake and threaten to give way underneath my weight. His broad chest human heaves with each breath, and his dark eyes are locked onto mine. My body is caught in the liminal space between fear and desire. The minotaur's gaze seems to penetrate me, the weight of it pins me in place.

"Little human," he rumbles, his voice deep and resonating.

His rough hand reaches out, brushing a strand of my hair away from my face. It's an unexpected tenderness from a creature so imposing, and the gesture warms me, even as it disarms me.

"Surrender to me," he murmurs, his breath hot against my ear, the scent of earth and musk filling my nostrils.

The air around us seems charged, every breath I take filled with the electric energy that flows between us. His eyes hold a fierce intensity that dares me to look away, but I cannot. I am captivated, entranced by the promise of pleasure and pain that glimmers within their depths.

So he doesn't want to chase me or hunt me down like the orc. He wants my surrender freely given even though we both know he could just take it.

"I submit," I breathe, my voice barely audible even to myself. "Show me what it means to be claimed by a beast of El."

A slow, predatory grin spreads across the minotaur's face, and he grips my waist with one hand while the other tangles in my hair. He pulls me closer, breathing in my scent as our bodies press together.

I feel his massive cock between us, still covered by his loincloth. He takes my hand and snakes it under his covering, placing it on his massive cock. It pulses and throbs in my hand, hot and thick and rigid. I grip the shaft, trying to swallow its width in my small hand. I'd need both hands to encircle it completely. The minotaur growls and tugs at my hair, yanking my head back with a snarl.

My back is arched, my chest thrust forward as I stare into his fiery eyes. My pussy clenches and my nipples harden, aching for the beast's touch.

"Beg me," he commands.

"Oh, God," I whisper.

"Beg me," he repeats, the rough grip on my hair tightening.

"Please, please, please fuck me," I plead.

"Who do you belong to?"

I pause, the question catching me off guard. "You," I whimper.

He uses a horn to hook my nightgown, rending it apart in one savage pull. I gasp as cool air caresses my skin and his warm body curves against mine.

My nipples stiffen and swell, and he bends his head to take one into his mouth, nipping at it with his teeth.

I cry out at the sharp sensation, aching for more even, reveling in his claim. He sucks hard, alternating between pain and pleasure as he pinches and pulls on my aching nipples.

I feel my pussy throb as wetness begins to dampen my inner thighs.

The minotaur growls against my breast, my hand still rubbing his cock, and he removes the loincloth, showing me a minotaur cock for the first time. It's thick and dense, a dark red. Veins pulse along the shaft, and I know it will be heavy with his seed. He's all girth, like a heavy club.

I stare at it in awe, enthralled by its size.

"Suck me," he rumbles, his voice deep and commanding.

Not needing to lower to my knees because of his height, I lean forward, wrapping two hands around the bull's dick just above the dripping head.

I feel the pulse of his cock like a second heartbeat in my hand. My tongue tentatively hooks into the slit of his cock head. A salty taste fills my mouth, and I indulge in the musky smell of his cock.

I lick the head, swirling my tongue around it as I begin to stroke him.

I pause and look up at him. "I've never done this before," I tell him. "Forgive me if I'm not very good...I want to please you."

"You please me, little human," he rumbles, his strong hands cupping my head as he presses my face to his warm body, then pushes me back to my task.

I continue to work his cock, sliding my mouth down his shaft as far as I can, which isn't far, taking in his warm flesh, feeling it grow and harden more with each passing moment.

My hands slide up the shaft, my fingers sliding along the pulsing veins of his cock, and I weigh his testicles in my hands, the heavy sack sits warm and full.

The minotaur growls and groans as I suck him, his hands tightening in my hair, his body tensing and quivering.

"I'm going to seed your mouth, little human," he rumbles, his voice deep and gravelly. "It's going to coat your tongue and fill your throat. You are going to drink my cum and you will know who you belong to."

I moan, my pussy clenching at the very thought of his hot seed in my mouth. I whimper around his cock, unable to speak with such a full mouth.

The minotaur growls, his hips thrusting forward, his cock swelling in my mouth. My lips stretch wide, and I feel his cock begin to pulse and throb, hot streams splashing against my throat and tongue.

I swallow his offering as much as I can, the salty liquid filling my mouth, my throat. The taste floods my senses. It is warm as it slides down my throat, filling my stomach, hot and thick.

He pulls out of my mouth and taps my cheek with his cock, his seed splashing on my face. I groan in pleasure, rubbing the head of his cock against my face, smearing the hot cum all over me.

I'm entranced. I'm...I'm such a slut. And I'm one hundred percent fine with it.

The minotaur reaches down, his hands cupping my breasts, and I shudder. He pinches and twists my nipples, sending jolts of electricity to my pussy.

He snorts and stamps his hooves, then roughly bends me over a nearby stone ledge. My hands grip its cold, jagged surface, and I brace myself for what is to come.

The minotaur wastes no time in asserting his dominance, positioning his throbbing cock at my entrance and teasing me with the large circumference tip. I whimper, shifting my hips impatiently, desperate for the fullness but worried he'll split me in two.

"Patience, little human," he murmurs, his hot breath fanning across my neck as he nips at it gently.

Every cell in my body screams for him to take me, but I force myself to remain still, allowing the anticipation to build until I am trembling with need. The minotaur chuckles darkly, no doubt sensing my impatience and delighting in it. And then, without warning, he thrusts into me with a force that leaves me breathless.

"Ah!" I cry out, the sound echoing through the labyrinth as the minotaur drives himself deeper inside me. My nails dig into the stone ledge, seeking purchase as he sets a brutal pace. The pain of his size is quickly replaced by an all-consuming pleasure promised me when I agreed. I welcome each powerful stroke with eager moans.

"Tell me you're mine," he demands, gripping my hips hard enough to leave bruises. "Say it!"

"I-I'm yours," I stutter, my voice barely audible over the wet sound of our coupling. "Please, don't stop."

"Little human," he rumbles, his thrusts becoming more insistent. "I will fill your horny womb with my seed. I will fill you with my cum, and you will come for me again and again. I claim you, little human."

His words send me into a frenzy, and I rock my hips back to meet him, welcoming each thrust. Having felt alone and misunderstood my entire life, being claimed means even more than I thought it would reading my precious books.

I belong. I am worthy. I have purpose.

I feel his cock swell, and I know that he is close to releasing his seed.

"Come inside me," I moan, arching my back as I feel his cock begin to pulse. He swells, throbs, and then he roars, and I cry out as his hot seed pumps into me.

"Yes," I gasp, my body trembling, "Breed me."

The pressure builds inside me and I come.

And come.

I begin to sob when my orgasm doesn't subside. It's too much. Lasting too long. Wave after wave of pleasure washes over me, as the minotaur continues to thrust into me, his cock pulsing, his hot cum filling me.

My body bows with pleasure as I moan and whimper.

And then, finally, the sensation begins to recede. My body relaxes, and I go limp in the minotaur's grasp.

He grabs my hair, pulling my face to his cock.

"Clean me," he demands.

My eyes are locked on his cock, his seed sliding down it. I move my tongue over his length and lap it up, taking in the musky scent of the bull. I taste both of us on my tongue.

When he moves away from my mouth, I slide to a heap on the stone-cold floor to rest. A new sensation thrums beneath my skin, echoing the beat of my heart and the hum of the labyrinth around me.

A hand strokes my hair, and I sense Mavius.

"Once again, you have exceeded my expectations, my little human slut."

My body trembles, my mind slipping into a haze of pleasure and surrender at both the praise and the degradation. The minotaur is gone. He didn't even say goodbye.

"I've never... I've never felt like this before."

"So eager, so willing to submit," Mavius growls, his voice rumbling through me like thunder. "You were meant for this, Alison. To be taken by creatures, to experience pleasures your human world could never offer."

"Y-yes," I stutter, feeling the warmth of his approval wash over me. It is intoxicating, this newfound understanding of my desires. "Thank you," I whisper.

He sits on the stone floor next to me and pulls me into his lap tenderly. "You're a fucking mess. Covered in bull semen."

I practically purr. "I know. This is the best dream, Your Majesty."

He chuckles darkly.

As I drift, I hear him speak of my transformation. It's almost complete. I don't follow what he's saying. I'm so very sleepy and his lap is so comfortable.

"ALISON, YOU LOOK WEARY. Please, feel free to use my chambers to refresh yourself," the dark prince suggests, his voice a smooth baritone that I could listen to all day.

I need to stop thinking this way. He's basically my pimp.

And then I'm no longer naked in the labyrinth with Mavius, but instead I'm naked in the doorway of a luxurious room. Alone.

"Thank you, Mavius," I reply aloud, though he's not with me any longer.

I really can use a rest.

The scent of spices and leather fills the air. The room is opulent with rich tapestries adorning the stone walls. A mammoth plush bed covered with velvet and satin dominates much of the space. Towering bookshelves filled with countless volumes of ancient tomes and what look like occult relics grace two walls.

It's his room. I can tell by the way it *feels*.

The adjoining bathroom is twice the size of my dorm room and is dominated by a bathtub that could probably seat four.

Yes, thank you, I think I will.

As soon as I think it, the tub fills with steamy water. Rose petals float on the surface.

Magic.

I quickly step into the waiting embrace of the luxurious tub. The warm water envelops me, soothing my aching muscles. I lean back against the curved edge, allowing the water to cover me completely, and close my eyes.

My thoughts drift, tangled and chaotic, as I try to make sense of all that has happened since I arrived in this strange world of El.

Am I already pregnant with the baby of one of the monsters? Will I return to my human realm or live here in El? Most likely, I will wake up soon to the alarm on my phone. I can't seem to decide if any of this is real or I'm dreaming.

I sense when I'm no longer alone. I lift my gaze, my heart pounding as I meet Mavius's eyes. He stands at the edge of the tub, a vision of dark beauty, his gaze filled with curiosity and desire.

"Forgive me," he murmurs, his voice low and seductive. "I couldn't resist the temptation to see you like this." Reaching for a sponge and dipping it into the warm water, he asks, "May I?"

His question hangs in the air, an offer that promises both intimacy and vulnerability. I hesitate for a moment, torn between my growing attraction to him and the realization that I'm still very much under his control. But the allure of surrendering to his touch is too strong, and I nod, granting him permission.

"I'm not allowed to tell you no, after all."

For some reason, my answer makes him look sad.

He begins to bathe me, his fingers deftly working the sponge across my shoulders and down my arms. I lean into his touch, careful to mind his claws.

"How are you holding up, little human?" Mavius asks, his sponge now trailing down my back, eliciting goosebumps across my skin.

His question catches me off guard, forcing me to confront the complexity of my emotions. "I... I don't know," I say, my voice trembling. "There's a part of me that craves their touch, their dominance. But there's also a part of me that fears losing myself in this world. I know that this is all about sex for them, and it's supposed to be about sex for me too. But, I feel like I'm missing something. It's probably a girl thing, but I sort of wanted more of a bond, I guess."

Mavius sighs, his fingers moving to massage my neck, sending a shudder of pleasure through me. "You don't find them mindless monsters then?"

As he speaks, his hands continue to glide over my body, his touch both soothing and electrifying. And in the midst of this sensual trance he's putting me in, I wonder what it would be like to surrender completely to him— to embrace the pleasures that the dark prince has to offer.

"No, not at all. Am I supposed to?"

As Mavius and I continue to talk, a subtle change begins to take hold in his demeanor. His voice lowers, becoming more guttural, the once-smooth lines of his face shifting into something rougher, more primal. I watch in fascination as his refined features morph before my eyes, his body growing larger and more muscular.

"Are you...?" I begin, unable to finish the question, my heart racing with a mix of fear and intrigue.

He grimaces, gripped in pain. "I'd hoped to...control this. I'm sorry...Alison...for what's about to happen," he replies, his new voice sending shivers down my spine.

"What—are you alright, Your Highness?"

"Cannot...pro...protect you from this."

His body convulses, his muscles bulging and contorting as his bones crack and shift beneath his skin. His nose and mouth protrude, forming a snout filled with gleaming, pointy teeth. Tufts of fur sprout from his skin, covering his body in a sleek coat of midnight black.

The transformation is both beautiful and terrifying. In a matter of seconds, the elegant dark prince is replaced by a snarling wolf-like creature. As he stands before me, upright like a human, his eyes glowing with a feral intensity, it's clear that I'm in danger. Mavius was always nearby during my encounters with the orc and minotaur. Who will protect me from Mavius?

"Are you afraid, little human?" he growls.

He lunges forward, pinning me against the side of the tub with one massive paw. I gasp, both in fear and excitement, as his hot breath washes over me. His eyes lock onto mine, and I can see the wild desire burning within them. I am at his mercy, completely vulnerable to his power.

"Let me go!" I cry, my voice breaking as I struggle, my slick wet body finding no purchase to get out of the bath. His powerful grip is both terrifying and arousing, making me shiver in his arms as he yanks me out of the bath and carries me to the bed.

The beast throws me onto the bed with a ferocity that sends shockwaves through my body. I skitter away from him, but trap myself at the headboard. His eyes burn into mine, a feral hunger that I've never seen before. My heart races as he prowls toward me, climbing onto the bed and crawling on all fours, his massive frame casting a shadow over me.

I try to scramble away, but he quickly catches me, his teeth bared in a snarl, his hot breath on my skin, his powerful body pressing me down.

"Please," I whimper, my voice barely above a whisper. "Please don't hurt me."

The beast growls, his eyes flashing with something that I can't quite understand.

"Mine," he snarls. He's salivating.

He leans in, his snout brushing against my neck, and I can feel the rough edges of his fur against my skin. My stomach flips at the sensation, part of me wants to push him away while the other part wants to submit to his power.

His sharp claws graze the curves of my breasts, causing me to gasp at the mix of pain and pleasure that courses through me. His dominance, previously subtle when in the form of Mavius, consumes him entirely now, and I am unable to look away from his lupine gaze.

I gasp and try to push him off me, but he is too strong. His teeth bite my breast painfully as punishment, making me scream in protest as a small rivulet of blood trails down my body.

He flips me roughly onto my stomach, my frightened cries met with his angry growls.

I should have been more careful what I wished for alone at night in my lonely dorm room. I regret it now.

At least, I should.

I attempt to squirm away from his grasp, and his teeth bite my ass, another punishment. He pulls me up hard by my hips, the now unsheathed oversized cock hot and hard against my inner thighs.

"Breed," he growls into my ear, driving the point home as he slams into me hard.

The pain is immediate and intense, overshadowed by the immense pleasure. God, such pleasure.

He pulls out, slamming into me again and again. With each thrust, the pain is quickly replaced with intense rapture. He pulls me back by my hair, his teeth sinking into my shoulder, his claws digging into my hips.

"Oh, God," I squeak.

My lust overtakes my fear and my body begins to buck against his. My toes curl and my stomach tightens, pleasure pulsing through my body, sending me into oblivion.

He stops thrusting in and out of me and holds me still while a strong pressure inside me grows. My vision goes white.

"Knot," he moans.

I cry out in protest, the pressure too much. My chest heaves as I try to catch my breath but I'm unable to. Everything is moving too fast. I can't think straight.

The knot is huge and foreign, throbbing inside me. My arms flail as I struggle to escape, so he slams me into the mattress and holds me there, his cock pulsing inside me.

"Careful," he warns. "You'll tear." He pulls me close to him, his tongue lapping at the bites on my shoulder.

I realize that he's trying not to kill me, that the knot locking his penis inside me will hurt me if I try to pull away now. I take a deep breath and do my best to relax, to stop struggling.

He howls, a terrifying sound, blasting a hot jet of his seed into me like a firehose, and I spasm, my body jerking in his grasp. Pain and pleasure mix, making everything feel more intense as he floods me with his seed.

My inner muscles spasm around his cock, squeezing and massaging it, milking him. My orgasm is so intense that I feel like I'm going to blackout.

We go on this way for a very long time.

I'm not even sure how I'm still conscious. Finally, he collapses on top of me, burying his snout into the crook of my neck.

Mavius begins changing again. I feel the fur receding, his face in my neck changing. We're still locked together by the giant knot in his cock, but he gently rolls us to the side so that he's spooning me.

"Are you hurt?" he asks, his voice a mix of Mavius and beast.

"I'm..." How do I even answer that?

"The knot will recede in a bit. It's important that you relax a little longer."

I nod. I'm too spent to struggle anyway.

The dark prince soothes me with gentle strokes. He does not degrade me this time. He does not call me a slut. He holds me like I'm precious to him as his cock continues to leak into me.

Eventually, the knot recedes and he pulls out of me. The sudden rush of wetness between my legs startles me. His seed trickles down my thighs.

"Do you hate me now, little human?" He's still holding me close. Still, caring for me.

"I don't hate you."

"You should."

I roll to face him. "Why?"

"I thought I could keep that particular monster at bay. I promised you I'd keep you safe so you could explore your fantasies, and I failed you."

"Was I in real danger then?"

"Yes, little human. You were in danger. I was in danger. It is my nature to want you to suffer for being mine. It's my nature to punish you for..."

"For what?"

"Wanting anyone who wasn't me."

Does he mean the monsters he told me to fuck? "I don't understand."

"Which part don't you understand, Alison?" He brushes the hair from my face. "Foolish girl. Your prince is a monster."

"My prince?"

"Ever yours," he says so matter-of-factly that my heart stops beating. "I thought I could keep that beast locked inside me, but I should have known. The minute I laid eyes on you, I wanted you. I wanted to claim you. I wanted to devour you. And I did." He looks away then.

"You...why...when...why did you want to breed me to all the others..."

I stop.

I recall the orc, the minotaur.

"It's you," I whisper.

I was so distracted by their cocks that I didn't see it. Not until now. I raise my hands to cup his face and he flinches from my grasp.

"It's you."

"You need another bath. We should clean your wounds..."

I push him onto his back and straddle him, peering into his eyes. Looking. Searching. "You are the orc. You are the minotaur. Why?" He's been shifting shapes since I arrived in the realm of El.

"How did you—?" he asks.

"Your eyes. Not the shape or color, but...something about your eyes."

He looks away. "You are a mess of blood and semen. Let's get you into the tub."

"You can't distract me. Tell me why? Why did you pretend to be them? Why did you command me to fuck them?"

"You wished it," he says so softly I can barely hear him.

"I wished it?"

"I watched you wishing it. I heard you screaming for it."

"When?"

"Your dreams. You dreamed of a monster, and well, I am a monster. I'm the worst kind of monster. And I dreamed of a mate." He pauses. "If you don't stop wiggling, I will fuck you again."

I don't understand any of this. "What is El? Am I dreaming this?"

"Perhaps we both are."

He won't answer me with anything more than riddles.

"What is your true form? You can shift to what...anything?"

"My true form is the monster I have no control over."

I AWAKEN SUDDENLY, disoriented, my fingers gripping my pillow tightly as the tendrils of my dream slip away.

I sit up and look around.

No. It can't have been a dream.

The vivid colors and sensations of El recede, leaving me with an aching emptiness. My heart is heavy with longing for Mavius, the enigmatic dark prince who ruled my subconscious nightscape.

The boring beige walls mock me. Of course it was a dream. I don't belong on El any more than I belong at this school. Mythological beasts don't need to rip off my clothes and breed me any more than guys my own age do.

Who was I to think that a prince or anyone else would want me so desperately that they would set up elaborate fantasies just to get me off...and then in a fit of rage, turn into a ravishing beast at the thought that I fucked someone else. Even if it was really him?

Seriously. The whole thing was stupid from page one.

The familiar weight of my mundane life settles back on my shoulders. My life has returned to monochrome.

Dragging myself out of bed, I prepare for the day ahead. I try to convince myself that it was just a dream, but there's a part of me that stubbornly clings to the hope that it was more than that.

In class, I struggle to concentrate on the professor's droning lecture, my thoughts constantly drifting back to the vivid memories of my time in El. The world outside my window seems so dull and colorless compared to the vibrant landscapes of my dreams—lush forests filled with strange creatures and ancient ruins teeming with secrets.

"Alison," the professor calls out, snapping me back to reality. "Are you going to answer?"

"Uh..." I stammer, frantically trying to recall what she had been saying. "I'm sorry, could you repeat the question?"

The professor sighs, disappointment etched on her face, and I feel the heat of embarrassment creeping up my cheeks. She repeats the question, and I manage to give a half-hearted response before sinking lower in my seat, wishing

I could disappear.

Throughout the day, I find myself lost in thought, reminiscing about my encounters with the mythological beings from my dream.

As the day drags on, I try to shake off these thoughts and focus on the present, but the memories of El—and Mavius—continue to haunt me, whispering seductive promises of adventure and pleasure just beyond my reach.

My stomach growls, reminding me that it's time for lunch. I trudge through the mass of students. Nobody looks at me, as usual.

As I enter the cafeteria, the scent of overcooked vegetables and greasy fries assaults my senses. Settling at a table near the corner of the room, I try to force myself to eat, but each bite tastes as bland and lifeless as my reality.

God. I need to work on this life thing. I can't live for reading romance novels and hoping I'll have naughty dreams when I go to sleep.

Over the din of the cafeteria, I catch snippets of a conversation from a group of girls nearby. They're gossiping about a new man on campus—someone irresistibly attractive, seen walking with the dean earlier today.

"Total hottie," one of the girls says, her voice dripping with excitement. "He's supposed to be some kind of expert in mythology or something. His last name starts with an M. Marvus or Marius. Something like that."

My heart skips a beat, and I nearly choke on a mouthful of tasteless salad.

That seems highly improbable.

The rest of their conversation fades away when they get up from their table.

Could this new professor or whatever he is have something to do with the dark prince from my dreams? And if so, what does his existence mean for me? Why is he at my school?

Maybe I saw him or read about him in a bulletin or something, and my subconscious turned that into a dream. A very surreal, strange dream.

After classes, after another tasteless dinner, I'm trying to study in my room but the hallway is crazy loud. Music is blaring from my neighbor's room, the bass thumping through the walls. I peek out the door to see a group of students congregating around her open doorway, talking and laughing loudly. There are empty beer bottles and pizza boxes strewn across the hallway, filling the corridor with the scent of stale booze and greasy food.

I feel a pang of envy as I watch them having fun without me. I want to join in but know that it would be pointless—they're all strangers to me. They probably wouldn't even notice me if I were there. I obviously didn't rate an invite.

I turn back to my textbooks, but the noise only gets louder. I can't concentrate. I look longingly at my eReader, but think better of it. I should wean myself away from my favorite escape before it breaks me completely.

If I'm not already broken.

With a sigh, I push myself up from my desk and throw my textbooks into my backpack. The library is open late on Fridays and not exactly a popular destination for college students who have already started their weekend.

Usually, there is a student working at the circulation desk, but tonight it looks like a man. He looks up as I approach, and our eyes lock.

"Good evening," he says smoothly, his voice like velvet wrapped around steel. "How can I help you tonight?"

His tall, imposing figure leans against the desk, his dark hair framing a face that could have been sculpted by the gods themselves.

A face I know intimately.

"U-um, I was just l-looking for a quiet place to study," I stammer, unable to tear my eyes away from him. He probably thinks I'm such a dork. He's good looking enough that I bet most of the students at an all-girls school have similar reactions.

But still. It's *him*. It's my Mavius. He's older looking, and he doesn't have black eyes or claws at his fingertips. But it's him.

But he doesn't recognize me. What is he doing here? None of this makes sense.

"Are you sure you have no need of me?" he asks, his eyes roaming over me with an intensity that leaves me feeling both exposed and exhilarated. "I must admit this place is too quiet tonight. My student worker was ill. I wouldn't normally be here at this time of night. It's only my first day."

"You're…"

"The librarian."

Trying to act casual, I say, "I'm Alison." I wait to see if my name registers on his face. Nothing. Nada. Nope. "You are?"

"I don't like formalities. I tell students to call me Joe."

Joe? What the actual fuck?

Okay, the Mavius I know would never in a million years tell anyone to call him Joe. Mavius loves formalities.

"I'll just..." I don't finish, instead making a beeline for a table. As I settle into a chair and attempt to focus on my textbook, I can't help but steal glances at "Joe." Each time I do, I find him already watching me. My heart races, and my skin tingles with an electric charge.

He's not looking at me like a friendly librarian looks at a student. But he's not making any allusions to me being his toy either.

Is he playing some kind of game with me? Or is this man's name really Joe? What am I supposed to do? Ask him if he remembers me? Ask him, "Hey Joe, does your penis have a mating knot in it?"

This is crazy. Nothing makes sense.

"Alison," Joe calls me from across the library. "Would you mind coming up here for a minute? I have something for you."

I approach the desk warily. It's possible that I'm suffering some kind of mental break and Joe is going to witness some banana pants crazy shit.

Joe leans across the circulation desk as if sharing a secret. "I have something that might be of interest to you." He reaches under the desk and produces a book that looks very old. "This is for you," he says, his eyes never leaving mine.

I accept the book hesitantly, an involuntary shiver sweeps down my spine as our fingers brush against each other. "Why are you giving me this?" The weight of the book in my hands feels like both an invitation and a warning.

I look at the cover. It's some kind of bestiary of mythological creatures. My gaze flies back to him.

"A good librarian knows how to match the perfect book to each patron. I have a feeling about you."

I swallow hard. "Do you know a lot about mythological creatures, Joe?"

"I'm familiar with them, yes," he replies slowly.

"I have some questions. Are you an expert?"

The smile he gives me is wolfish. "I'm an expert in many things. What would you like to know? What would sate your appetite for knowledge?"

I pause. He's not giving me much to go with yet. But the Mavius I know also speaks in riddles. "Are there any mythological creatures that can enter your dreams?"

"Quite a few, Alison."

"Are they monsters, Joe?"

His eyes darken but do not turn black. "Oh, yes."

An alarm on his phone sounds. "It's ten o'clock. Time to close up the library."

He goes to the doors and locks them. I watch the familiar, graceful way he moves. "Are you going to collect your things? I'll let you out."

I can't leave this library without knowing.

All my life, I have been shy, been an outsider. I had an amazing experience in El, and if I don't come away from it changed, what was the point?

If I want a different life, I need to do things differently.

"Do you know what the library stacks remind me of?" I ask.

He looks perplexed by the question. "I haven't a clue."

"A labyrinth."

A miniscule twitch on his jaw is my only reward. "You're right. It can be like a maze in here."

I start up the stairs to where the stacks are.

"Alison, where are you going?"

"I need a book."

"The library is closed...Alison, come back."

I reach the top of the stairs and begin running through the shelves of books hoping he will come find me rather than call campus security.

"Alison, where are you?" he calls.

I listen carefully for his footsteps and then dart across an aisle. Suddenly, I feel his warm breath on my neck. "You're a naughty girl, Alison," he whispers.

I spin around to face him, my heart racing.

"Joe..." I say breathlessly. I take a few steps back.

Joe moves closer, his eyes holding mine. He speaks in a low voice. "You're not supposed to run in the library."

My breath catches again. I take another step back, but he follows me, closing the distance between us.

"Is this what you wanted? A merry chase with a man too old for you? A man who is charged with educating you? I've seen your kind before. All innocence in your plaid schoolgirl skirt, fooling no one with what's hot and needy beneath it."

"I'm sorry."

"I don't think you are. I think you wanted to tempt me with forbidden fruit. I think you wanted to turn a good man into a beast."

One of his hands reaches out to caress my cheek, the gentle touch with his hard words putting me off balance.

"Do you know what a labyrinth is, Alison?"

"I have some experience with them, yes," I say hesitantly.

He grins, taking my hand and tracing a finger along my palm, causing me to shiver. "It's an ancient symbol for self-discovery," he says in a low voice that sends tingles down my spine. "But it can also be a place of danger, where one can lose themselves, never to return."

I open my eyes and stare at him, my heart pounding in my chest. "What are you trying to say, Joe?"

He leans in closer, his lips brushing against my ear. "I'm saying that sometimes, the only way to find yourself is to lose yourself completely," he whispers.

Suddenly, the book in my hand feels like a weight, pulling me down to the floor. I drop it and wrap my arms around Joe's neck, pulling him closer.

"You're being naughty again, Alison."

"Tell me about it."

"I could lose my job."

I still don't know if he's my dark prince or if he's really "Joe."

"In all my years of working in universities, I've never crossed the line with a student," he tells me.

I walk my fingers up the front of his shirt, stopping on the first button. "Are you tempted by me?"

He grabs my hand and stops it from going any further. "Yes. Of course, but we shouldn't."

I pout. "I'm a very lonely girl, Joe. Don't you want to help me?"

"Alison..." he says regretfully.

Fuck. Is he really not Mavius?

Then he slams my back against the shelf, lifting my legs around his hips so I feel him in my center. "Is this what you want? You want to be taken by an older man, used roughly in a public place?"

I nod, my breath coming out in shallow gasps.

"You want me to break the rules?" he asks, his voice gruff.

I nod again, and he leans forward, pushing himself against me. I can feel his heat through the fabric of his clothes and it's making me ache for more.

He kisses my neck, biting gently before whispering in my ear. "You don't even know anything about me. I could be a monster."

"I'm counting on it."

I undo Joe's pants and grasp him firmly.

"I've never met such a hot little slut," he tells me, pushing my panties to the side. "You're so fucking wet."

He's got his fingers in my pussy and I'm using the bookshelf behind me as support. "If you were a mythological monster, Joe, what would you be?"

He stops fingering me. "What?"

I give him a squeeze. "Tell me what you are."

"Every man is a monster, Alison."

I think I might have made a horrible mistake.

"ARE YOU OKAY?" HE ASKS me. Now I know he can't be Mavius. Mavius doesn't stop to ask if I'm okay.

I've just...come on to the new university librarian like something out of a bad porn scene. And his fingers are in my pussy and his cock is out. I can't exactly say *whoops* at this point. Plus I'm so horny.

Joe plunges his cock into me hard. Wheezing for air, I remember too late that I'd only dreamt I lost my virginity to an orc. My hymen is still very much intact.

Was.

"Ow, ow, ow."

"You can take me."

There's no immediate pleasure to replace the pain in this realm, but it begins to get easier.

"You're mine now," Joe says as he thrusts into me. "Mine to do with as I please. I can have you whenever I want. You can't say no to me."

I grunt in response.

"Say it," he commands, thrusting faster.

"I can't say no to you."

"Tell me you're mine."

"I'm yours." I'm about to come.

"Say my name."

I shake my head.

He slams me against the shelves. "What did I tell you about saying no? Say my name."

I tug his hair. "Mavius!"

"What did you call me?"

His cock swells, the knot locking us firmly in place.

"Mavius," I repeat, my voice trembling. Thank God.

He smiles. "That's right. You belong to me, Alison. And I'm never letting go. Come on my cock, little one."

He puts his thumb on my clit and I'm lost. "Mavius," I gasp as my orgasm takes over.

He leans in, whispering in my ear. "I'm going to come in this tight little pussy."

He grunts and thrusts into me one last time, spilling inside of me.

We both collapse onto the floor, his knot still trapped inside me.

He pushes the book I dropped toward me on the floor. "Look up *Mavius* in the book."

"Now?"

"We've got time to kill." The knot inside me twitches to remind me I'm not going anywhere.

I awkwardly thumb through the tome and read:

Mavius, the shapeshifter demigod of dreams, is a creature of great power and mystery. According to legend, Mavius was once a demigod who was bitten by a werewolf and subsequently banished to the realm of El for his careless mistake.

In El, the land of dreams, Mavius became a master of shape-shifting, able to take on any form he desired. He is said to appear in the dreams of mortals, tempting them with his seductive nature and whispering secrets in their ears.

Mavius is also known to possess the ability to manipulate reality within the realm of dreams, shaping the very fabric of the dream world to his will. He is a being of great intelligence and cunning, and his motives are often shrouded in mystery.

Some legends suggest that Mavius is not content to remain in the realm of dreams, and that he seeks to break free and wreak havoc upon the waking world. Others say that he is a benevolent being, offering guidance and wisdom to those who seek him out in their dreams.

Whatever the truth may be, Mavius remains a figure of fascination and fear, a being whose powers and motives are not fully understood by mortal minds.

"How exactly does a demigod get bitten by a werewolf?" I ask when I finish reading. "Aren't demigods, like, super powerful or something?"

"To be fair, she was a very lovely werewolf. But I was careless."

The knot has receded, and he is able to pull out of me. His seed leaks out of me and onto the floor.

"How are you here if you are banished to El? Am I dreaming this too?"

"No," Mavius says, shaking his head. "I can move between the two realms if I wish. I'm not limited to just El. The book doesn't know everything."

I scoff at his derision of books, my beloved and only friends. "Why did you come in the form of a librarian?"

He begins idly playing with my breasts. "Your fantasies were not always about monsters. You had a naughty professor binge not too long ago. "

Heat stains my cheeks. It's disconcerting that none of my private dreams are private. "Why me? Why choose me for all this?"

"I didn't choose you, Alison, you chose me. You reached out to me in your dreams and I answered," he explains it so matter-of-factly when it is anything but.

"What do you want from me, Mavius?"

"The same thing I've wanted from you since we first met. I want you to explore the realm of El with me. I want you to experience a world beyond the one you know. I want a mate."

"How does this work? Do you just show up in my life in random bodies? What if I want to be with the real Mavius?" *Is there a real Mavius?* "Wait. You bit me in El. Am I going to be a werewolf now?"

He sits up. "Those are a lot of questions. I shall endeavor to remember them all."

"You're sounding awfully haughty, Joe," I tell him.

"Minx. No, you did not get pregnant or get a real bite in El because you were only partially in El, your body remained here. However, I could have bred you just now as both our bodies are in the same realm." I gasp, but he keeps going. "And if I bite you when you are not dreaming, it's likely that you will also carry the curse. As for how this *works*, if you don't come with me, I suppose we could continue to meet in your dreams. But I can't visit this realm in person too often. Your kind are not ready to mix with mine." I look at him strangely, and he answers, "You are special, Alison. How many times do you need to hear that from me?"

I sit all the way up and hug my knees, his cum still leaking out of me onto the library floor.

"What are you thinking, little one?" he asks tenderly.

"That I'm scared. But I don't know what scares me the most. I think that it might be that you will leave me here, and I'll never see you again."

Am I ready to leave the human realm completely? The only family I have left sent me to this school to get rid of me. My parents are gone. I have no friends. The only thing I would miss is my eReader, and there are plenty of books on El from what I saw in his room alone.

And if I'm pregnant, wouldn't I be better there than alone here?

But Mavius is dangerous. He's manipulative and could obviously bite me at any time and turn me into a werewolf. I don't even know what that means in terms of everyday life. Would a child be safe in El with two werewolf parents?

"You think louder than any human I've ever met."

"How many humans have you met?" I ask, feeling a little jealous.

"Scads. You're the only one I've liked, though."

Well, that's something.

"If I come to El with you, will I be in danger?"

He takes my face in his hands. "Not from anything on El, my love, except for me, of course. You will be my mate, and I will protect you from anything and everything. If you choose to stay with me, I will ensure that you have a long, happy life full of adventure and magic."

"And if I'm pregnant?"

"Then the child will be protected by both of us." He smiles. "You will never be alone, Alison. I will always be with you."

"And if I'm not pregnant?"

He smiles wolfishly. "Then I shall fuck you until you are."

So My Parents Sacrifices Me to an Orc

SELENA HAS BEEN SICK for five years with a mysterious disease that no doctors can diagnose, much less treat. As her teen years turned into adult years, nothing seemed to help. Desperate, her parents turned to alternative remedies and finally an internet witch.

That's when things get weird.

According to the witch, the only cure for Selena is the ejaculate of an orc. Since orcs don't exist, this should be a problem, right? That's what Selena thinks when her parents have her taken deep into the forest and left in a cave. She's sure she'll die there. Until she realizes she is not alone in the cave. She's been given to a monster.

The orc, Bryxan, understands the assignment and immediately begins administering Selena's very special *treatment* plan. Several times a day. Will the unorthodox remedy heal Selena? And if so, what happens when it's time to leave the cave of the humongous brute she's accidentally fallen in love with?

Author Confession: If you've made it this far in the collection, you'll sense a theme about what happens when monsters spread their seed inside young women in the forest. It's called breeding, y'all. Good luck, Selena!

YOU KNOW IT'S GONNA get weird when your parents consult with an internet witch for alternative treatment for your mystery illness. You know they are desperate when they agree to leaving you in a cave. With an orc. For his *cum*.

Yes, Lydia the Internet Witch convinced my parents that not only is there really such a thing as an orc, but his ejaculate will magically heal my mystery sickness that has me wasting away.

The illness started five years ago when I was fifteen, and no doctor has had any success in diagnosing what is wrong with me, much less treating me. So my parents started searching alternative treatments. Herbs. Crystals. Cryptid semen.

I am wearing a white nightgown that looks like something you would see on the cover of a gothic novel from decades ago. I have been deposited in the mouth of a cave in the middle of the woods. I am the only person who thinks this is not only weird as fuck, but also dangerous. I'm not afraid of an orc, because they are not real. But I am afraid of bears, wolves, cougars, and banjo playing mountain men who haven't seen a woman in too many years to count who might happen upon me in the forest wearing nothing but a sheer white nightgown.

I know my illness has caused my parents to crack, but this is a lot worse than I thought.

Lydia has assured them that she will *psychically know* when it's time to come and get me after my treatment. So now I wait and hope I don't fucking die from the elements (or bears) before whatever this illness is can kill me.

Orc cum. Seriously.

If there were such a thing as an orc, this means my parents are fine with me doing the nasty with him. I've seen illustrations of orcs. They are huge. And green. And not friendly. But sure, give your daughter to one. By all means.

I'm tired. Well, all the time. And I ache everywhere. Also all the time. I don't think I will live through the night out here by myself. I sit against the cave wall and close my eyes. Maybe if I have a little nap, I can hike back out on my own (right). Find the highway (sure). Flag down someone who hasn't lost their freaking mind to help me (absolutely).

That's when I hear it. My heart rate kicks up a notch.

Breathing. *Heavy* breathing.

It's a terrifying sound, raspy and deep, coming from the depths of the cave. I hold my breath and my body stiffens, eyes wide in the dark. There's something in here with me. Orc? Bear? Crazed mountain man? All equally terrifying options.

My eyes flash open, my entire body rigid as I peer into the deep dark. Instinctively, I shiver and withdraw further into the corner, watching as the dominating figure lumbers closer. It's a human-like silhouette, large and broad, with a rugged outline that doesn't look anything like a person. Or a bear.

"Human," the figure grunts, his voice sounding like two boulders grating against each other—the deep timbre resonating through me in a way that's terrifying. "Say name."

I strain my eyes to make out his features, but in the dim light of the cave, all I see are sharp teeth glinting and tusks.

Orcs are...real? Fuck my life.

"S-Selena," I stutter out, my voice barely above a whisper.

"Se-lena," it rumbles, the word rolling off a thick tongue and echoing through the chamber. The figure lumbers closer, the ground shaking beneath his massive weight. Now, only a few feet away, I can make out more of him—the rough, green skin, prominent tusks, and massive build.

Oh my God.

"Bryxan," he announces, thumping his chest in a primitive show of identification.

I nod, unable to meet his gaze, my voice weakening with each passing second. "Bryxan," I echo, a tremor shaking through me as I utter the name.

"Selena sick," he says after a moment, and I blink in surprise at how he senses my illness. His large hand reaches out, hovering over my body as if he's afraid to touch me. "Bryxan help."

I glance at his hand, then up at his face, an explosion of questions detonating in my mind. "How?" is the only one that manages to escape my lips.

Bryxan growls low, a rumble that seems to shake the cave. But then he's quiet for a moment, as if considering his words. "Orc seed," he says finally, his voice grating over the words.

This cannot be happening.

"No," I protest. "I should go. Home. I should leave. I don't want to bother you. Or your seed. I'll just scuttle away now."

But Bryxan just grunts and hauls me up over his shoulder, turning back the way he came.

And taking me with him.

What I thought was a normal cave turns out to be more like a cave facade of a much more elaborate dwelling. Bryxan carries me through a network of tunnels, the walls of which seem to pulsate with a living light, casting an ethereal glow over everything. We finally arrive at a chamber, the center of which holds an enormous bed of soft furs.

In the next moment, my nightgown is gone, stripped away by the hulking orc in one swift tear. My naked body is laid out on his bed, the touch of fur is soft against my bare skin. My cheeks flush with embarrassment at my nakedness, but Bryxan's attention is solely focused on securing my wrists and ankles with thick ropes.

Securing me with rope. Oh my God. What is happening? I mean, duh. I guess I know what's happening. But did I hit my head or something? This is so surreal.

"Bryxan..."

"Hush, little human." His voice is a deep rumble that sends vibrations through the bed and into me. "Bryxan help."

In the dim light, I watch him remove his pants. His large, muscular body is covered in rippling green muscles. His manhood is impressively fierce looking, and it's dripping with pre-cum. Panic flashes inside me.

I watch as Bryxan takes himself in his hand, his movements slow and deliberate. An orc cock is hard to describe. It's thick, veined, and gleaming with a natural sheen that seems almost incandescent in the dim light. He focuses on his task with an intensity that is both confusing and, to my surprise, wildly arousing.

Especially considering that the diameter of that cock would tear me in two. And I'm naked and tied up.

As he strokes himself, I try to look away, but can't. He's not gentle with himself at all. His efforts gain momentum, rough and unapologetic. His grunts fill the chamber, echoing off the stone walls until they're the only sound I can hear. I can't help but squirm under his gaze, my body responding to this in ways

I've never experienced before.

Bryxan climaxes. Thick ropes of his silvery semen shoot across my body, covering me in a warm, viscous cream.

"Bryxan, what..." My question dies on my lips as he starts to rub his cum into my skin with his large, rough hands. The sensation is electrifying, a strange blend of shocking and soothing. It's as if the very essence of him is seeping into my pores, filling me with a strange warmth that chases away the constant chill I've been feeling.

I scrunch up my nose as the heady scent of his potent cream fills the air. It's bizarrely alluring, musky and earthy with a hint of spice that is distinctly him. It is the scent of raw, primal masculinity and it awakens something deep within me.

Bryxan's ministrations become more focused, his immense fingers swirling around my navel and gently sliding between my thighs. My breath hitches and a wave of fear washes over me.

"Please don't," I say. My voice sounds small and weak, but there's a hint of something more. A questioning curiosity.

His fingers land on my clit and I gasp, taken aback by the unexpected contact. He rubs his cum over it, spreading the warmth. A moan slips from my lips as he continues to glide his thick digits in slow, deliberate circles. My body responds ardently, my hips rolling with his movements. The room is filled with the sound of our heavy breaths intermingling.

The sensation builds, my body burning with an overwhelming heat that I can't ignore. It's as if all the energy in the universe is concentrated in that one spot, spiraling outwards in sparks of pleasure.

I'm pulling against the restraints, the rope biting into my wrists as I writhe and squirm under his touch. The intensity is building, overwhelming in its ferocity. My lungs burn for air as I pant and gasp, the sounds echoing off the walls of the cave.

Bryxan doesn't stop. He keeps moving his fingers, the texture of his rough skin and the slickness of his cum driving me to the brink. My moans grow louder, each sound ripped from my throat, each one more desperate than the last. The pleasure swells within me, a building storm that threatens to tear me apart.

I shudder and stiffen as I climax, my body convulsing under his massive hands.

"Little human rest now," Bryxan says, his voice a soothing rumble that reverberates through me. His hand continues to move slowly, gently, riding out the waves of my orgasm until I lay limp and sated.

The ropes around my wrists loosen as he unties the knots, his massive fingers surprisingly dexterous as they release me from my bindings. There is an unexpected tenderness in his actions, a gentleness that belies his monstrous appearance. His green eyes meet mine, and for the first time, I see what might be a hint of concern seeping through.

I'm embarrassed. I just got doused in orc juice and came like I've never been touched before (which unless you count my own hand, I haven't been). My eyes are so heavy, though. I can't stay awake, no matter how hard I try.

I sleep hard, I don't know for how long. I wake up to another massage, the scent of Bryxan's cum wafting through the air again as he spreads it over my skin.

My body feels different, rejuvenated somehow, like I've been plugged into a source of primal energy, seeping into my bones. Bryxan is silent, his focus entirely on his task. His hands working across my skin, the fresh layer of his thick cum soothing away the earlier aches and pains.

This is ridiculous. It can't really be happening.

Orcs don't exist. And if they did, their jizz wouldn't be healing to a human woman.

Right?

Chapter Two

I STIR AWAKE AND FEEL a sticky residue on my skin. I guess it wasn't a dream.

Memories of the previous night flash through my mind as I sit up and look around, holding a fur to my chest to cover my breasts. Why? I don't know. He's seen everything I have to show.

Bryxan is sitting nearby, his piercing black eyes watching me with a mixture of curiosity and concern. Next to him, a spread of fruits and nuts on a makeshift table, a simple breakfast prepared by my orc.

The Orc of Much Cum.

After feeding me, Bryxan picks me up and carries me deeper into the cave. Naked. Still. If you're keeping track.

"Not very talkative, are you?" I ask.

He grunts.

We stop in a chamber filled with strange artifacts and symbols. It feels spiritual in here. Like this is his church. His altar. I'm honored, I guess is the word for it, that he brought me into it.

He shows me a mural on the cave wall depicting an Orc warrior protecting a smaller figure. Like a human maybe? Like me? Does Bryxan see himself as my protector? I reach out to touch the mural and my fingers trace the rough lines of the warrior's form, feeling the power etched into the stone.

Bryxan watches me, his gaze heavy. He points to the smaller figure, then at me, clearly indicating our roles.

"Yes, Bryxan. I see it," I say softly.

He grunts again, a low, rumbling sound that seems to serve as his form of agreement. He takes my hand and leads me out of the chamber to another part of the cave. It's a natural pool of crystal clear water. Steam rises in gentle plumes from the bubbling surface.

Bryxan strides forward, shedding his rough clothing until he stands before me in all his naked glory. His body is a testament to strength and endurance, his muscles starkly defined beneath the emerald green of his skin. I can't help but take him in, my eyes drifting over the hard planes of his chest and down to his abdomen, the powerful length of his legs. My gaze lands on his member, half hard, and a flush spreads across my cheeks. He merely watches me watch him, no shame present in his features.

Well, what does he have to be ashamed of? He's so well made, so muscular and virile. His body is an artwork of primal strength and masculine beauty.

And when exactly did I decide a humongous green man with tusks is beautiful?

He dips into the water, his large frame disappearing beneath the surface like a powerful sea beast. His head emerges and he shakes it, sending droplets sprinkling around him. The steam from the water billows around his form. He looks at me again, those animalistic eyes piercing my own with an intensity that makes me feel like prey. Maybe willing prey, but prey all the same.

With a gentle tug, he pulls me into the pool, the warm water lapping against my thighs. He's careful as he guides me to a ledge of smooth stone, a natural seat in the water just deep enough for the heat to soothe my aching body.

He sits across from me, his eyes never leaving mine. The steam rises between us, weaving an ethereal veil that does nothing to hide the pure intensity in his gaze. It's a curious mix of things—devotion, concern, desire—all rolled into one compelling stare. I've never been looked at this way before.

"Selena sick," he says. "For long time?"

I nod. "Yes. I have been unwell for some time. Nobody seems to know why. Or how to help." I roll my shoulders, realizing I do feel a little better than I did yesterday. "You are trying to heal me. With your...seed?"

He nods. "Some humans need orc."

"Do some orcs need humans?"

He pauses, his gaze unwavering. His eyes flicker down to my chest and back to my face before answering in that deep rumble of a voice, "Some do." The implication hangs heavy in the steamy air between us.

His powerful hands break the surface of the water and he reaches out to me, tracing the ridge of my collarbone delicately. His touch sends ripples of pleasure coursing through me, igniting a warmth that centers on the point of contact and spreads outwards, curling around every nerve ending. I look at him, eyes wide. He merely nods, as if understanding the turmoil within me.

"Humans and orc not always believe in other."

Well that's true enough. I didn't believe in orcs before yesterday.

"Orc seed healthful to sickness," he continues. "On skin also inside. Inside female, yes?"

Inside. He means...I swallow at the implication, my throat suddenly dry despite the steamy air around us. The look in Bryxan's eyes confirms my understanding, but there's also a question there—a silent plea for my consent.

My heart thuds loudly in my chest as I contemplate the prospect. It's not what I would have ever imagined doing before this moment, but there's a strange sense of trust building between us. I look down at his large, green hand against my pale skin, surprisingly gentle.

"Little human fearful. Orc seed not scary. Inside and outside, help sickness faster. But little human want only outside okay too. Inside heal faster, but outside fine."

I blow out a breath. "I'm not afraid of your...seed. But your..." I gesture below the water and then hold my hands out about twelve inches apart. "Big."

"Bigger than human male," he boasts, his chest puffing out with pride. An unexpected chuckle escapes me, and he grins in response, his teeth sharp and stark against the dark cavern, but not unkind.

"Size not matter," he continues, the grin fading but leaving a soft gentleness in his eyes. "But orc take care. Not hurt little human."

Right. Size doesn't matter. Sure. I don't think many human women were built to take an orc that big. But especially a woman who is...well, me.

"I've been sick a long time, Bryxan. Since I was a teenager. I didn't have a chance to date." He looks confused, like my words don't make sense. "I've never been intimate." Nothing registers on his face. This is humiliating. God. "Selena untouched by male," I finally try.

Understanding dawns in his dark eyes. A strange silence hangs between us, the only sound is the steady drip of water.

"Selena first time...with orc?" he asks, a sense of awe in his voice.

"Yes," I murmur, not trusting my voice to speak any louder.

A brief silence stretches out between us, making my heart pound even louder in the echoing quiet. The scent of him fills my senses—earthy, musky and surprisingly comforting.

He rests his massive head on the ledge behind him, studying the cave ceiling like he's looking at night stars. "Orc fuck hard. Not easy on little human." He clenches his jaw. "Challenge to not tear in half."

I gasp. "Byxan, you are not helping!"

He shrugs. "Truth." He studies the ceiling some more. "Some females like rough fuck. Maybe Selena?"

My turn to shrug. This is so awkward. "I don't know what I like. Other than not being torn in half."

"Seed on outside of Selena maybe best. Not fast. Maybe Selena drink orc also."

If I didn't already feel better than I did yesterday, I would finish this discussion with a no thank you. He's going to keep coming all over me, and now I guess I'm supposed to blow him. Did my parents think this through?

"I'm not sure about 'drinking.'"

"Challenge Selena." That he says this with a very naughty grin makes my pulse quicken. Is it strange that I actually find this massive orc intriguing? Attractive, even? The thought brings a flush to my cheeks, and I quickly look away.

"Selena like challenge?" Bryxan's voice rumbles in the low-lit cave, snapping me out of my thoughts.

"Yes," I reply, holding his intense gaze. "I like a challenge."

He grins then, a wolfish flash of his teeth. "Good," he rumbles, stroking the rough pads of his fingers against my cheek. "Orc like Selena spirit."

His touch, so warm and surprisingly gentle for such a massive creature, sends a wave of tingles through me. I gulp, unsure what I should do next.

"Hope Selena hungry."

BRYXAN CARRIED ME BACK to his bed, I think sensing that I was tiring again. He's arranging me gently on the furs, but not tying me up this time.

"Bryxan, why did you restrain me yesterday?" I ask.

"Selena want rope?"

I shake my head. "No! I mean, I was just wondering why."

He shrugs. "Selena scared. Might run. Not run today."

He's right. I might have fought him harder yesterday. I trust him more now. So fucking weird.

"Can tie Selena again. Some females like."

"No thank you."

"Selena said she doesn't know what she like. Maybe Selena like restrain." His words are very polite, but the look in his eye is anything but.

"Perhaps," I answer, a hint of uncertainty coloring my voice. "Perhaps not."

He chuckles, a deep sound that rumbles within the cave walls. "Selena find out. Soon."

That dark promise sets my heart racing. It looks like now he's getting ready to administer the same "treatment" as yesterday. He never put his pants on after our soak, and his giant orc cock is getting...more giant. And kind of glowy.

He's going to paint me in orc seed again. And this time, I am anticipating it.

"Ready?" Bryxan asks, his rough voice sending shivers down my spine.

I try to look brave, but I know I can't hide the trepidation in my eyes. Still, I nod and whisper, "Yes."

He grins at me again, this time his eyes soft. "No hardship to come all over pretty little human." He takes his cock in his hand and begins a languid stroke, his eyes locked onto mine. It's an oddly intimate moment, despite the strange circumstances.

His pace is slow, deliberate. He seems to savor each pull of his hand, quietly groaning in pleasure. The sight is hypnotic, terrifying, and incredibly erotic. I can't tear my eyes away from him, my gaze fixated on the powerful strokes of his hand on his massive length. His eyes meet mine, a challenge and a promise in their fathomless depths.

"Selena watch," he commands, his gruff voice thick with arousal. My breath hitches at the raw power of his words, the authority ringing in his tone. I barely manage a nod, my heart thudding in my chest as I keep my gaze locked on him. "Selena aroused. Can scent."

I squirm at the implication, but he's not wrong. I am aroused, my thighs are wet with it. My cheeks burn.

Bryxan grins at me, his tusks glinting in the dim light of the cave. "No need feel shy," he says. "Makes more seed churn for lovely Selena. Scent of Selena make Bryxan harder."

His strokes become faster, more urgent. His thick, orcish groans grow louder and begin to echo around the walls. My hips undulate unconsciously, drawn in by the erotic sight before me. I watch as Bryxan's muscles tense, and his face contorts into a grimace of pleasure. An intense climax shatters through him, his seed spilling in hot spurts across my body.

I gasp as the warm liquid hits my skin more forcefully than yesterday. He holds his cock over me and sprays me from my chest down. Before he's even finished, I'm rubbing it into my skin, massaging the cream into my breasts, my stomach. It smells so good, and he's not done yet. He keeps stroking his length, grunting and groaning with each spurt. "Good girl...healthy Bryxan seed for Selena," his voice husky and thick with satisfaction. I watch in fascination as he continues to milk himself, beads of his seed pooling on my breasts.

"Here," Bryxan commands in a low voice, taking my hand and guiding it to his still-hard length. "Rub cock on lips, little human. Taste on tongue.

A shudder of anticipation runs through me as I wrap my fingers around his warm, veiny length. The skin of his cock is softer than I expected, a contrast to the roughness that makes up the rest of him.

Under his watch, I bring his engorged member to my lips, gazing up at him with wide eyes. "Drink," he murmurs, his breath hitching as my tongue darts out to taste him. He tastes better than I could have imagined, a faintly sweet and salty flavor that sends tingles rushing through me. I tentatively lick at him again, my taste buds awakening.

His rumbling growl of approval spurs me on, and I open myself wider, taking the head of him into my mouth and sucking what still dribbles out. Drinking him.

Too soon, he pulls away from my face and massages his cum into my skin.

I'm vibrating from the feel of him, the taste of him.

"I need..."

"Orc take care of human." He palms the head of his still wet cock and squeezes. How can there still be more in there? He brings his now wetter fingers to my core. "Open legs," he instructs, his voice a low, gravelly rumble.

Without thinking, I obey. His fingers, slick with his essence, trace the sensitive folds of my heat. A gasp rips from my throat as he swipes at my nub. My body arches off the makeshift bed in an instinctual reaction, my fingers digging into the coarse fur blanket beneath me. He massages his essence onto me, using it as a salve and applying it with gentle, painstakingly slow strokes. I'm slick and needy and begging him, "Please..."

One of his fat digits stretches me, dipping inside my heat. The sensation is foreign, yet not unpleasant, a sweet ache that spreads through my lower body. His thumb continues to work against my pulsating bud, creating a dual sensation that has me gasping and writhing beneath him.

"Human need orc," he murmurs. "Selena need Bryxan."

In the dim light of the cave, Bryxan's eyes look like dark glittering jewels. His fingers still inside me, he leans in closer, his breath warm against my skin. "Bryxan need Selena," he rumbles, and I feel the vibrations of his words against my sensitive flesh. The deep resonance stirs a flutter in my belly, a sweet torment that spreads from my center to every inch of my body.

"Bryxan," I whisper, and he rewards me with a low growl, sending sparks of desire shooting through me.

A low keen escapes my lips as he stretches me further, his thick digit pressing deeper. The ache is sharper now, but the pleasure quickly absorbs it. His thumb circles my clit at an agonizingly slow pace and I buck against him, reaching for more.

He uses his free hand to grab my breast roughly, squeezing the flesh and thumbing the hardened peak. A jolt of pleasure sears through me, so intense that it leaves me gasping for air. He pinches my nipple hard, sending another wave of delight cascading down my spine.

"I want...I want..." I stutter, but the words escape me.

"Selena like a bit of rough," he proclaims, pinching my nipple again and sending a sharp spike of pleasure straight to my core. "Bryxan give," he rumbles in answer.

His thick digit moves within me rhythmically, a maddening tempo that promises release but keeps it agonizingly out of reach. And then he bites the tender flesh of my inner thigh, a sharp pang of pain that surprisingly morphs into incredible pleasure. I cry out, my hips jerking towards him, begging for more. I feel him smirk against my flesh, his tusks lightly grazing my sensitive skin.

Orgasm seems too polite a word for what happens to me. It's like dying one thousand times and coming back to life one thousand and one. If he were not holding me down, I would have bucked him off me. My body jerks and shivers, my muscles clenching around his invading finger. His name tears from my throat in a wild scream that echoes around the cave.

The world blacks out for a moment before it comes back slowly, colors fading back into focus as I blink open my eyes. Still panting, I find him watching me with an intense gaze, his dark, fierce eyes soft with a tenderness I'd never seen in anyone before.

"Sleep, Selena."

And I do.

I'M NOT SURE HOW WE can walk around the forest and never come across another human being, but we do. Byxan believes the fresh air is good for me, and who am I to argue. It's day four of our time together and I'm filled with more energy than I've had in years.

I don't think it's the fresh air, though.

Several times a day, I'm doused in orc seed. Always finishing with a few long pulls of his cock in my mouth. He makes me come, and then I rest, eat, bathe, and we do it again. With occasional breaks in the woods. He obviously loves nature, pointing out different trees and plants and birds, giving me their orc name and what humans call them.

He has fashioned me some leather slippers so I can walk without cutting my feet, and he wraps me in fur when it gets chilly. In the small suitcase my parents left with me, I have found only more white nightgowns and a toothbrush. I assume I am some kind of maiden sacrifice to the wild orc of the forest.

I kind of like being a maiden sacrifice so far.

We're sunning on a flat rock near the river, his sizable chest propping my back, his muscular legs bracketing me. Keeping me safe. I feel small and protected. And something...else.

Maybe it's gratitude. I don't know. It feels stronger than that. I'm for sure grateful. Grateful for the birdsong and the sun and the way my health is improving because he's helping me. But my feelings about him are muddled by an undercurrent of something deeper, an axis around which my world has begun to rotate.

It's not gratitude. I really like him. I care about him.

His warmth radiates from behind me, his quiet strength resonating like an unseen force field. The language barrier between us isn't insurmountable, but I feel like we communicate without words so much of the time. Sometimes I feel like we share an invisible thread of understanding.

His fingers trace idly up and down my bare arm, causing goose bumps to rise on my skin, but it's a welcome sensation. We're silent for a while, just soaking in the serenity of nature. We watch together as a small, lively bunny hops curiously around the periphery of our sun-soaked patch of earth. I can feel the deep vibrations of Bryxan's laughter against my back as the rabbit scampers off into a thicket, its fluffy white tail bobbing in its wake.

He likes small, cute things. He often chuckles at my antics, too.

I turn, sitting on my knees, and face him.

"Small human need something?" he asks.

I study his face carefully and bring one hand to his cheek, tracing his jaw gently. He's become...unbearably handsome to me in a short time. An orc. Handsome.

The ridges and valleys of his face have become familiar to me, and I find myself drawn to the wildness within him. "May I touch your horns?" I ask.

His eyes narrow slightly, a look of surprise flashing across his rugged features.

"Selena touch orc?" His deep voice rumbles out softly, the husky tone going straight to my core.

"If it's okay."

Slowly, he nods and leans closer, his hot breath tickling my cheek as he dips his head to give me better access. His horns are a prominent part of him, dangerously different from humans. But I'm not afraid of them anymore.

My fingers find their way to the base of one, tracing the rough surface with tender curiosity. I can feel his breath hitch slightly, a small indication of what I can only decipher as pleasure. They are not smooth as I imagined, but have ridges and crevices that my fingers explore with awe. I lean forward, pressing a soft kiss to the base of one horn.

He inhales sharply, his muscular arms tightening around me in a reflexive embrace. His surprise tastes sweet to me. I like knowing I can unbalance the giant orc.

I can feel the tension in his body, but instead of pulling away, he allows me to continue. My lips trail from the base of one horn to the other, my hands cradling his face tenderly as I explore this new aspect of our relationship. This new intimacy.

His breath quickens beneath my touch, my kiss, a shudder running through his massive frame like an earthquake when I nibble his earlobe. And then suddenly, he's pulling me into his lap.

"Enough," he growls, but there's a softness in his gaze that wasn't there before.

"Did I do something wrong?" I ask, heart pounding.

"No," he rumbles, his hands sliding up my body, creating a path of heated desire. "Too much. Too sweet."

His confession hangs in the air between us. I take his giant hands and put them down on the rock, telling him with my eyes they are to stay put. I lean toward him, nuzzling the patch of skin just below his ear, and I inhale. I believe he has several patches on his body that carry extra pheromones or something. I suckle gently, ignoring his grunt, and move my kisses down his body. His shoulder. His pectoral. When I get to his nipple, I graze it with my teeth and he hisses.

"Bryxan likes a bit of rough," I say, parroting what he told me the other day.

His eyes flash with surprise and a bit of amusement, but he stays obedient, hands firm on the rock as I explore his body. I repeat my actions, nipping at his other nipple. His body tenses under me, a low growl rumbling from his chest.

"Yes," he admits, his voice strained. "Rough."

I let my hands roam lower, tracing the cuts and ridges of his impressive abs, my fingers dipping into the crevices. I glimpse movement out of the corner of my eye and realize Bryxan's hands are clenching and unclenching on the rock as if he's battling an internal war.

As I move lower still, his muscles tighten even more under my touch, the bulge in his loincloth becoming more prominent. My fingers graze it experimentally, heart hammering in my chest as I study his reaction. His eyes are on mine, heavy with desire and something else. Confusion?

I discard thoughts of uncertainty and focus on him, my hands pulling away the fabric acting as his loincloth. His impressive length leaps free, hardened and dripping, the sight of him leaving me breathless.

Always breathless.

I trail a single finger from base to tip, enchanted by the texture of him, rough yet silken. A bead of his essence pools at the tip, and I collect it with my thumb, eyes meeting Bryxan's as I slip my thumb into my mouth.

"Nutritious and delicious," I whisper, a sly smile teasing at the corners of my mouth. His green skin flushes a darker hue, his jaw clenched tight as he watches me with hooded eyes.

"Selena plays with orc," he complains.

"Orc will live. Selena promise."

Beneath his sizable green cock are his balls, and I've not had much to do with them yet. That's where he makes the seed that is healing me, and I feel a sense of curiosity about them.

After he comes on me during our treatments, the sac is usually drawn tight, almost hidden in the coarse dark hair of his groin. But now, unsated and lusty, his balls hang heavy and full, intriguing in their alienness. I cup them tentatively, weighing their warm bulk in my hands.

He lets out a shuddering breath, his molars grinding as he clenches his jaw tightly.

Taking that as encouragement, I let my fingers dance over the soft, velvety skin, my touch light but exploratory.

"Selena like?" he asks, his speech tight and strained.

"Selena likes very much."

I push him onto his back so I have more access to his balls. Nuzzling the sac, I realize this is another patch of skin that secretes the pheromones I am so addicted to. I want to worship him here, the place where his seed is made, the seed that has brought me back to life. My tongue traces a wet path over one, then the other, savoring the unique flavor of him, my hands firmly stroking his length. He twitches under my touch, a low growl emitting from his throat.

"Will you drink?" he asks. I'm surprised at his use of the pronoun "you" more than the request itself.

Usually, I've taken from his cock only after he's come all over me, but never when he's at his most likely to spray like a firehose. I'm mentally trying to figure out how to unhinge my jaw for this undertaking. But I want to feel him in my mouth. My throat.

"Yes," I answer. I begin with licks and kisses, exploring every ridge and vein of his impressive length. I can hear the deep, guttural sounds he makes, each one encouraging me to continue. My tongue teases the swollen mushroom tip, tasting the pre-cum already leaking from him.

He tastes so good.

I become bolder, taking more of him into my mouth. His hand softly threads through my hair, his grip firm but not forceful. Even in the throes of pleasure, he is mindful of his strength. My rhythm is slow and steady. It has to be due to his size.

As my mouth works to pleasure him, I feel the tantalizing anticipation of his release. The scent of his desire fills my senses, driving me to quicken my movements. I can really only get the head of his cock in my mouth, but his grip tightens in my hair, a signal that he is close already.

My jaw aches, but the steady stream of pre-cum keeps me driven, keeps me wanting more. The taste of him, rich and salty, is addicting. I want it all.

A low growl echoes from him, vibrating through his body and into mine. "Selena," he groans, his grip in my hair tightening further. "Drink."

His command sends a shiver of anticipation spiraling through me, settling deep in my core. Bryxan thrusts one final time into my mouth, releasing a torrent of hot, potent seed that I eagerly swallow as he roars into the forest. The taste is stronger than the other times, more intense, but the sensation of nourishment is instantaneous.

Of course, I cannot keep up with the spray of his seed and I pull back, my hand replacing my lips as he continues to spill onto my skin. His creamy essence covers me, the feel and sight erotic and satisfying.

He's still spraying me, and my hands massage him into my skin. And then he pulls me up so my pussy is on his shaft. He shifts my hips back and forth, grinding me onto him as his hands cup my buttocks, fingers kneading into the flesh. I gasp at the contact, feeling his length rub against my wet folds, slick with my arousal. I moan out loud, lost in the rhythm of our mutual desire.

One of his fat pinkie fingers presses against my back entrance, and I gasp in surprise. But rather than fear or discomfort, a wave of pleasure courses through me. My initial shock turns into a soft moan as he slowly pushes his finger deeper, his other hand still guiding our slow grind against each other.

"Come," he commands, as his finger claims more territory inside me. The sudden pressure sends a bolt of pleasure racing through me. I shudder, breathless, my body crashing into an earth-shattering orgasm.

The world spins, yet I'm securely anchored in his arms. The exquisite sensation overwhelms my senses, each wave stronger than the last.

The orc continues his ministrations, not stopping until every fragment of my climax has dissipated. Once spent, I slump against him, my heartbeat echoing in my ears as I try to regain my breath.

Bryxan cradles me tenderly, fingers soothing the small of my back, a comforting weight against my hypersensitive body. We remain like that in silence, the sounds of the forest resuming around us, a natural symphony echoing our own primal rhythms. The scent of us, a mix of his musk and my release, hangs heavy in the air.

Chapter Five

WHEN I AWAKE ALONE in our bed the next morning, I'm confused. Usually there is a morning treatment that wakes me up.

I take care of my morning necessities and go off in search of the giant orc. Our intimacy in the woods yesterday has changed something in me. Something more than just my improving health.

I'm practically skipping around the labyrinth of the cave system. Each time we are together, it becomes less about me only taking from him for my health. I want to give as much as I receive. He deserves so much.

As I traverse the dimly lit paths, my heart flutters in anticipation. I feel the warmth of my anticipation to see him spread through me. I'm...happy.

Bryxan makes me happy.

But where is he? It's strange that I can't find him.

At the mouth of the cave, I poke my head out. Maybe he's outside. I step out, listening for him, and only take a few steps when I'm grabbed roughly.

"Little human stay in cave," he growls. "Still sick and weak."

I blink at him as he deposits me back inside. "I'm not feeling very sick or weak today. Where were you?" I playfully wrap my arms around as much of his waist as I can. "I missed you."

"Busy," he replies dully, unwrapping me from his body.

Something is wrong. Off. "Is everything all right, Bryx?"

"Bryxan busy."

But the set of his face is hard, his eyes averted. There's something he isn't saying, and his evasiveness feels unlike him. He's always straightforward, truthful even when it's too blunt. But now...

"Bryxan," I begin, tentatively reaching out to touch his arm. He doesn't react, and I'm left feeling a pang of worry. "Did... did I do something wrong?" I ask.

"No," he says, though there's a heaviness to the word. "Bryxan hunt. Selena stay."

He turns from me then, leaving me standing alone at the mouth of the cave. My heart sinks at the cold dismissal. I watch his broad back disappear down the path, till he's out of sight. I have never seen this side of Bryxan. He's always been so attentive, so gentle.

My nakedness feels suddenly shameful.

I find myself wandering back into the depths of the cave, my once light footsteps now heavy.

I've never had a romantic relationship with a human, much less an orc, so I don't know what I did wrong. Things were perfect yesterday. Weren't they?

My mind races, kicking up dust and uncertainty. Had I pushed too hard? Misread his intentions? Is he tiring of my company?

God. I'm stupid. So, so stupid. We don't *have* a relationship. I pushed for intimacy where there isn't any. Just because his "seed" is the treatment for my illness doesn't make us lovers.

To him, I am sick and weak.

I crumple onto the makeshift bed, pulling his fur blanket to my chest. Bryxan's unique scent clings to it, a mixture of earth, musk and spice. I bury my face into it, letting the powerful fragrance fill my nose.

Obviously, what I need to do is stop focusing on my love life and pay more attention to my healing. The sooner I am healthy, the sooner I can get out of his way. He's done so much for me, and I repay him by getting clingy and having a crush.

Stupid.

I get up, do some light exercises, things I remember from gym class before I got sick, and then eat some fruit and nuts he left out for me. A good soak in the warm spring will do me wonders, so I go there next. And then a nap. As I drift off, I remind myself that when he comes back to give me my treatment, I'm not to read too much into it.

No feelings. No tenderness. Sure, he's nice to me. Sure, he takes care of me. He's obviously a healer of some kind. He would do this for any woman that needed his treatment. Maybe that's what the cave drawings are about.

His calling may be foreign to humanity—coming all over your patients is something frowned upon in our medical field. But it's a calling to him. To tend to small humans. To make sure they eat, rest, get fresh air, soak in the healthy spring. And bathe in cum.

Alternative medicine, yes. But it's working.

I will push back my own arousal. Let him come on me, take the last of it in my mouth like usual, but that's where it stops. I will not let him make me come also. My pussy is not his concern. I won't force him to make it more intimate than it needs to be.

My resolve wavers as I hear the familiar sound of his footsteps approaching. The sight of him sends a jolt of mixed emotions through me, but I detach my feelings, steady my breathing and maintain an impassive expression. Bryxan looks at me for a moment, then wordlessly unties his rope belt, letting his trousers fall to the cave floor. His cock springs free, proudly on display and ready.

Does he have to think of something else, someone else, to get him hard so he can come? Or does orc biology make him always ready for his human burden?

My heart hammers against my ribs, my body begging me to touch him, to draw him closer. But I swallow back my desires, reminding myself of my earlier resolution.

It's just medicine. That's all this is between us.

As I sit up, I can't help but notice how his black eyes soften momentarily before he steps toward me. With deliberate, slow movements, he begins to stroke himself in front of me, his hand moving rhythmically over the length of his impressive orcish member. The sight of it sends heat flooding through me, and my mouth waters in anticipation. But I hold myself still, focusing on the task at hand.

After a few moments, Bryxan lets out a low growl, deep in his chest, signaling his climax is near. Heat flashes through me, and I prepare myself for his release. He moves closer, standing tall over me. His hand is a blur now, the rhythm of his strokes quickening until with a deep, guttural roar, he releases. The hot, thick spray splashes onto my bare skin, a few droplets making their way into my open mouth.

"Thank you, Bryxan," I say coolly as I massage his life giving cream into my skin.

He looks at me with a confused glint in his eyes, but simply nods, pulling his trousers back up and securing them around his waist. He leaves without another word, and I finally release the breath I'd been holding.

With my heart still drumming loudly in my ears, I rub his seed into my skin, sucking some from my finger into my mouth since he didn't offer a drink. I am a mix of emotions—relief, confusion, and worse...unfulfillment.

But I won't touch myself. I don't need to come. I don't want to come. I need to detach desire from the process or I'll go mad.

I take a fur from the bed and create a little pallet further away so that he doesn't feel the need to share a sleeping space with me when he returns. If he returns.

I'm already so much better than I was a few days ago. Maybe I'm almost healed. Maybe the witch will get her psychic hit that I'm ready to be retrieved by my parents soon. I'll be able to put this all behind me and live a healthy life.

When I wake up, I'm being carried back to his bed.

"BRYX?" I SAY, CONFUSED, forgetting for a moment what happened between us. And then I remember how he closed off from me. So what is he doing now?

"Sleep, little human," he says as he puts me back in his bed.

I stiffen and throw the fur off myself, scrambling away. Or try to. I don't get very far as his huge arm pins me to the pallet.

"Let me go!" I squirm, my voice trembling, but Bryxan just grunts in response.

"No," he says simply. His breath is hot on my neck, and I can smell the earthy aroma of his skin. His grip doesn't weaken.

"Get off of me."

"Sleep."

"You insufferable brute," I spit, trying to wriggle out from under his arm. But Bryxan doesn't move, his grip remaining firm but not painful.

I feel his erection on my hip, and I lose my shit. "This is not okay," I shout, pushing against his chest. But his chest is a wall of hard muscle, immovable and unyielding.

"Quiet," he rumbles lowly, his hand moving from my waist to cover my mouth.

I try to bite his hand, but orc skin is tough. I doubt he even feels my teeth. Despair washes over me, and I stop struggling. I feel defeat rolling over me like a cold wave.

When he senses the fight has left me, he removes his hand, staring at me so long that tears well up in my eyes.

"I hate you," I say quietly.

"Good." He releases me, moving away slightly, though not nearly enough for comfort. I try not to think about the hardness still pressing against my hip, focusing instead on the emptiness inside of me.

Suddenly, it's too much ,and I turn away from him, waves of overwhelming shame and humiliation wash over me. I feel his gaze on my back, a silent question that I can't answer.

I can't believe I let myself fall for an orc. Who does that? Well, nobody because orcs aren't even supposed to be real.

I'm going to blame my circumstances. I didn't get the experience of dating and boyfriends in my teens because I was so sick all the time. I missed Boy School. Apparently books and movies are no substitute for experience. He's just my first heartbreak is all. All girls have at least one guy ghost on them at some point. Right?

But when a normal guy ghosts, they go radio silent. They don't come all over you and walk out of the room. They don't drag you back into their bed and hold you down.

Bryxan stays silent for a while, then his hand draws small circles on my back.

"You don't need to comfort me," I snap, not daring to look at him. His hand stills momentarily, but then resumes its gentle tracing.

His body shifts behind me, the heat from his skin radiating against my own. Then I feel the coolness of the room as he pulls away. I shiver, wrapping my arms around myself.

Hot and cold seems to be the general theme lately.

Why didn't he leave me on the small bed I made for myself? Why was he so nurturing for four days, and then just shut down?

It doesn't matter. I just need to get my rest so I get better faster. Ugh. But my mind won't stop spinning. Finally, I can't take it anymore.

"I promised myself I wouldn't ask. That I would have pride or whatever. You confuse me, Bryx. Maybe it's because orcs and humans are different. But you seemed to care about me, for a time. And then you just stopped. I thought you and I were something we weren't. And that's okay that you don't feel the same. But you could have found a nicer way to let me down."

He's silent for a long time, so long that I start to think he won't respond at all. But then he shifts again, turning me around to face him. His eyes sear into mine. "Orcs...talk...hard."

I nod. "Sure."

Fucker.

"Selena too sweet."

Oh, this is the orc version of "it's not you, it's me." Unless he really means I'm too sweet. Like, too nice or whatever. That orcs like tough warrior females or something.

Whatever. I'm not his type. Fine. I roll back over.

"Okay." What else can I say? Argue that I'm not too sweet?

"Bryxan not need sweet."

"Got it."

"But Bryxan...need Selena," he rumbles. "Bryxan...confused. Selena...make Bryxan feel different. Not bad." He pauses, taking a deep breath. "Bryxan try...Bryxan no good...with talk."

I roll over so we are facing each other again. "Bryxan, it's all right. I understand," I whisper.

He reaches up with one massive hand, guiding my hand to his hard chest. A low rumble resonates in his chest, and he presses my hand against his beating heart. "Feel?" he asks, his voice barely a whisper.

I nod silently, feeling the steady thump under my fingertips. It's strong and rhythmic, like a drum of war echoing across an ancient battlefield.

"Selena get better. Leave Bryxan. Bryxan heart not leave Selena."

Understanding dawns on me. He's not unlike many human men after all. We got close yesterday, and it scared him. Because he doesn't want to care too much and get hurt.

I take his big hand and put it on my heart. "Feel?" I ask, mirroring his earlier question.

He nods, his eyes never leaving mine as he feels the steady beat of my heart beneath his palm. I can see the realization dawning in his gaze.

"It hurt me, here, when you pushed me away today. I care about you. I'm afraid of my feelings too."

The furrow of his brow eases slightly, replaced by a look of surprise. Yet, there is also relief there. His hand pulls away from my chest to gently cradle my face.

"Selena...care?" His deep voice caresses the words, like he's tasting them, rolling them around on his tongue. I nod, smiling softly at the amazed expression on his face. "Bryxan... care," he says quietly, as if saying the words will make them more real.

His hands are gentle, hesitant at first, as they explore the contours of my face. His touch is soft and reverent, like he's afraid to break me or mar my skin with his rough hands.

My lips part instinctively as Bryxan's thumb brushes across them. His breath hitches at the sight, his eyes darkening with desire and need. "Selena," he murmurs, his voice husky with emotion. He leans closer, his breath warm and inviting against my cheeks. My heart races in anticipation.

His lips meet mine in a rough kiss, his tusks brushing against my skin. It's an odd feeling, yet not unpleasant. My breath hitches as I feel his arm wrap around me, pulling me into his strong embrace. The feel of his warm, hardened body against mine feels so right. His tongue explores my mouth with a primal eagerness that leaves me breathless, his taste rich and intoxicating. I mirror his actions, exploring the depths of his mouth with my tongue, tasting the raw, earthy flavor that is purely Bryxan.

My hands move over his broad shoulders and down his muscled back, tracing each rugged line and ridge of his physique. He grunts in pleasure as I rake my fingers down, reaching the firm curves of his ass, gripping them tightly. His body tenses and he pulls away from the kiss, his breath ragged. He stares down at me with a burning intensity that makes my heart flutter in my chest.

His fingers trail down my neck, tracing the curve of my collarbone before descending to my breasts. I gasp as he cups one with his large hand, thumb teasing across the sensitive peak. His eyes don't leave mine; they're dark and filled with a kind of raw hunger that sends heat spiraling through me. His touch is firm but careful, a contrast to the rough skin of his fingertips.

He bends his head down, his lips latching onto the sensitive peak of my breast that his thumb was just teasing. A gasp escapes my lips as he suckles, his tusks a surprising and electrifying contrast to the softness of his lips. I grip the back of his head, my fingers threading through his coarse hair, encouraging him to continue his ministrations.

His other hand slides down my body, tracing over my belly to rest on the curve of my hip. His fingers dig into my flesh, not painfully but with a firmness that holds me in place. I gasp as his thumb ventures further, stroking the sensitive inner folds between my thighs. His movements are slow and deliberate, heightening my anticipation. As his fingers find my most intimate area, I can't help but arch into his touch, a soft moan escaping my lips. The intensity of his gaze does not waver; he watches my reactions with a hunger that mirrors my own.

His fingers continue their exploration, finding the slick warmth that waits for him. A growl rumbles in his chest as he increases the pressure, circling the sensitive nub of pleasure nestled within me. An involuntary whimper slips past my lips, and I grip the furs beneath us, my knuckles white with strain.

"Selena very small here," he says, one fingertip at my opening.

I can't stop the blush that creeps up my cheeks at his words, but I nod. "Yes, Bryxan. I am."

He grunts in acknowledgement, and slowly, oh so slowly, begins to push a single digit inside me. I gasp, my breath hitching in my throat as he fills me with the thick pad of his finger. The sensation is deliciously overwhelming. I grip his arm, my nails digging into the hard muscle beneath his rough skin as I adjust to the fullness.

His touch is patient, allowing me time to adjust to the penetration before withdrawing his finger and pushing back in. It's slow and meticulous, each thrust going deeper than the last until I am whimpering and writhing beneath him, my hips bucking against his hand.

Then he inserts another digit, exploring my depths and stretching me. And I know what he's stretching me for.

I know that he is preparing me for him, for the fullness of his orcish girth. I shiver in anticipation, the idea of him being inside me sparking a bolt of arousal that shoots through my body. I whimper again, my fingers gripping into his arm as his fingers continue their intimate exploration, his thumb pressing against my clit with a steady rhythm that causes my body to jolt with pleasure.

"Good?" he rumbles, not stopping his motions even when I choke back a gasp and nod fervently. His thumb circles a little faster, a little harder, and I can't help but let out a squeal at the sudden increase in pleasure. My body tenses, my toes curling as I feel the familiar tightness growing within me.

Then he removes his hand. I blink, confused.

"Edge," he says simply and goes back to sucking my nipples.

Edge?

In the heat of the moment, it takes me a minute to understand his meaning, but as he pulls away, leaving my body yearning for his touch, I realize he's brought me to the edge of climax and is holding me there. The realization sends a heady thrill through me.

The straining ache of desire throbs through me, the need for release a tangible thing clawing at my insides. Yet, there's a wicked thrill in the denial, the knowledge that my climax is under his control, held within his massive hand like a precious gem.

His mouth returns to my breasts, his tongue swirling around my hardened nipples, his teeth nipping gently, each pull sending a delicious twinge straight down to my core. The tension within me builds further, my body straining towards its release, but Bryxan is merciless. He keeps me teetering on the brink for what feels like an eternity until I am begging him, my voice a pleading whisper begging for release.

"No," he rumbles, his voice like a dark promise, his tongue flicking out to tease me further. I can feel the anticipation building within him, the heat of his desire radiating off him in waves. He reaches between us, his hand wrapping around his hard length, his eyes never leaving mine as he strokes himself slowly. His orcish grunts fill the room, the sound low and erotic.

"Inside Selena?"

I nod emphatically, barely able to contain myself any longer. I watch as he brings it to my entrance, the head of his cock glistening with his pre-cum.

"Yes," I moan in encouragement, my heart pounding in my chest as he slowly pushes into me. The stretch is intense, the fullness overwhelming, and I let out a keening moan as he fills me, inch by agonizing inch.

His eyes are fixed on mine, a glint of something wild and primal within them. He waits, every muscle in his body taut as he gives me time to adjust. Then, he pulls out some before pushing back in, setting a slow rhythm that has me gasping.

Each thrust brings a new wave of pleasure, each withdrawal the sweet agony of loss. His powerful body moves against mine, his tusked mouth finding my throat, my breasts, my lips. I wrap my legs around him, pulling him closer, deeper.

What we must look like, the giant green monster and the delicate mortal woman intertwined in such an intimate embrace. His rhythm builds, pace quickening as his strokes become harsher, more desperate. The room is filled with the sluicing sounds of our bodies moving together, the primal grunt of his lust, my high keening cries. I can feel the pressure building within me, a coiling spring ready to snap. My hands clutch at his broad shoulders, nails digging into his thick green skin as I brace myself.

"Selena like a bit of rough," he grunts, a wicked smile playing on his lips. I can only respond with a desperate nod, my entire body alight with pleasure.

Bryxan does not disappoint, his movements becoming more frantic, more possessive.

He flips us over so that I'm straddling him, his rough hands guiding my hips as I ride him, my movements matching the rhythm he sets. The new angle has him pushing deeper, and with each downward thrust, I can feel every ridge, every vein of his thick cock. His fingers dig into my hips, holding me in place as I move against him, pleasure coursing through me like a wild river.

I look down at where his giant cock has split me open, and the sight only adds to the spiraling pleasure. His green skin against my pale pink flesh, his length disappearing inside me, then reappearing slick with my arousal. I grind down harder on him, chasing that delicious friction.

His rough hand slides up to cup my breast, his thumb grazing over the sensitive peak while his other hand maneuvers between our bodies. When his fingers find my clit, a sudden jolt of pleasure shoots through me and I gasp, my rhythm faltering for a brief moment. Calmly, persistently, he rubs the swollen bud as I bounce on him, his touch sending waves of pleasure coursing through me. I feel the coil tighten within me, my climax approaching, unstoppable.

"Bryxan," I gasp out, "I'm...I'm going to..."

He nods, grunting in response. His fingers move faster over my sensitive nub, his cock pounding into me with reckless abandon. His grunts become guttural, matching the frenzied pace of our bodies.

My orgasm squeezes his cock unforgivingly, and my vision blurs. My voice is lost in a strangled cry of absolute ecstasy, my body convulsing as wave after wave of pleasure washes over me. He grunts again, louder this time, his massive frame stiffening beneath me. His fingers dig into my hips, leaving marks that will surely color by morning. His low grunt morphs into a bellow, the sound vibrating through me, adding another wave to my still-rippling orgasm. I feel his cock throb inside me and then the hot rush of his cum filling me to the brim and spilling over.

The sensation triggers another orgasm, smaller this time but no less potent, and I shudder on top of him, his thick shaft still pulsing inside me as he empties himself completely. His hands, previously rough in their urgency, now become gentle as they guide my trembling body down onto his. We are slick with sweat and the remnants of our lovemaking, but neither of us cares.

The warmth of his body envelops me, the coarse texture of his green skin a comforting and familiar terrain under my spent body. I can feel his chest rise and fall beneath me, his breaths deep and heavy. He runs his fingers soothingly through my hair, tracing the curve of my skull. I close my eyes, surrendering to the blissful aftershocks, my body humming with satisfaction and the undercurrent of a new, strange connection. Bryxan's thumb gently caresses my cheek as he murmurs gentle words of praise in his native tongue, the roughness of the orc language strangely soothing.

He rolls me to my side and slides out of me, rubbing his slick cock on my belly before reaching down with his massive hand to gather some of the tumbling spill. He brings it to my lips, his green eyes piercing into mine as if asking for permission. I open my mouth, extending my tongue to taste us. Ingest us.

"Are you mine now, orc?" I ask him, smiling with spent desire, sated but not quite satisfied. Not yet.

His hulking form shadows over mine, his black eyes glowing with a fierce possessiveness. "Little human own giant orc."

"Giant orc own little human," I counter and he grins.

He leans down to kiss me again, his tongue sweeping across mine, mixing our shared tastes. It's a deep, languid kiss, filled with promise of more to come.

But as we fall asleep, I'm reminded that outside of this cave and this intimate moment, there are still challenges we need to face. Outside of this cave, a different world waits, one where Bryxan the orc might be feared and reviled, and where I might be despised for loving him.

And I do.

Love him.

THE WORLD SPINS AS I come to consciousness, the rough fabric of a blindfold pressing against my eyelids. My breath catches in my throat, and for a moment, I'm drowning in darkness. The hum of an engine vibrates through my body, and I realize I'm in a moving car.

"Where am I?" The words leave my lips in a panicked whisper, but no one answers.

I try to move, but restraints bite into my wrists, securing me to something cold and unyielding. My heart pounds against my rib cage, each beat screaming for escape. I strain against the bindings, but they hold firm, mocking my efforts with their unrelenting grip.

"Help!" The cry rips from my chest, desperate and raw. "Somebody, please!"

"Quiet down, Selena," A voice, gruff and emotionless, cuts through the din of my distress.

"Who are you? What do you want from me?" I demand, my voice shaking. The last thing I remember was fighting as the two human men were trying to pull me out of the cave. They must have drugged me.

"Your parents sent us," one of the men reveals, his tone matter-of-fact.

"My parents sent you to drug and kidnap me?"

"They sent us to rescue you. But you were fighting us, and we had to hurry. Couldn't risk the monster coming back."

"Please," I plead, my voice breaking. "You don't understand."

"There's nothing to understand," one man says, his voice flat. "We rescued you."

Rescued? Is that what they think?

I knew my parents would send for me again. Why didn't I plan for it better? The car engine hums, each turn and stop marking the unwilling journey back to my old life.

"Almost there," one of the men says, a hollow attempt at reassurance.

We pull into the garage of my parents' home. I guess so the neighbors don't see me getting out of the car all tied up and blindfolded. As they are removing the restraints, my parents rush into the garage.

"Selena, thank God you're safe!" my mother exclaims, engulfing me in an embrace that feels more like shackles than affection. "How do you feel? You look so much better. We feel horrible about what we put you through. We didn't know what else to do."

"But I was happy," I murmur, pulling away from my mother's suffocating hug. "The orc healed me, Mom. You and Dad did the right thing by sending me there."

Will they do the right thing by letting me go back?

"Selena," my mother pleads, her hands reaching for me, "please, don't hate us for sending you there. You must have been so scared."

Hate them?

My father hugs me but won't look me in the eyes. I think they both feel weird that they pimped me to a monster. They won't let me talk about my time in the cave. They're ashamed.

I'm not.

That night, I have dinner with my parents at the table instead of a tray in my room for the first time in years. I'm not used to feeling well. It's kind of a trip to be able to eat without feeling nauseous, to have this newfound strength and health. But with every bite that I take, every glance at my parent's concerned expressions, I can't help but wish they had left me in the forest.

I know my dad won't ever discuss that they literally sent me to a monster cave so an orc could jizz on me. We're going to pretend that it never happened. Much like the first few years of my illness when we pretended I had the flu.

I half expect Bryxan to bust through the wall like the Kool-Aid Man and take me back to his cave. I wonder what he thought when he got back from hunting and I was gone. Does he think I left him on purpose?

No one will entertain the idea of even discussing what happened to me in the cave. As the days go by, I find myself alone in my room more and more, staring out the window at the world outside. The walls of my room are a prison.

It's been two weeks, and Byrxan hasn't come. And no amount of internet research has explained the unexplainable to me. I can't even find any conspiracy theories about orcs or the healing power of their semen. I also can't get the witch my parents consulted to return my calls or emails. I don't know what to do. How to act.

Sometimes, I think I dreamed the whole thing.

It would be best for everyone if I just tried to be normal now. I need to figure out things like a career and if I want to go to college. My whole world is open again. My future bright. Instead of sickly, I'm now filled with vigor, life burgeoning within me.

And that is what I'm half-afraid is literally happening.

I haven't had a menstrual cycle in years, so I have no calendar to consult. But something feels different.

My body, once so frail and weak, now pulses with an energy I've never known. My breasts feel full and heavy, my skin glowing with a radiance that wasn't there before. But those full breasts? So damn tender.

My hands tremble as I grip the edges of the porcelain sink, staring at the reflection of a woman I barely recognize. I swallow hard, willing my racing heart to calm as I wait. The sharp beep of the timer slices through the silence, and I force myself to look down at the digital test resting on the marble countertop. Two lines. Positive. A surge of shock ripples through me, leaving my skin tingling with a mix of fear and exhilaration.

I'm pregnant.

How is this possible? I mean, duh, I know how it happened. But who thought two different species could breed? Can I even carry an orc baby to term? Deliver one safely? They must be huge.

Guess I'm going to find out.

I press a hand to my still-flat belly, warmth blossoming and flooding the crevices of my heart. A sense of protectiveness overcomes me. No matter what the consequences, this baby is mine. Bryxan's. Ours.

I laugh, a soft breathy sound that echoes in the quiet bathroom. It's crazy, so incredibly crazy. A baby? My baby? Bryxan's baby? A newfound sense of purpose flushes through me, filling me with determination.

In my heart, I know what I must do. I can't stay here.

There's a knock on the bathroom door. "Selena?" My mother's voice, tinged with concern, filters through the door. "Selena, are you alright?"

How do I explain to my parents what he means to me—what this child means? They haven't wanted to hear one thing about my time in the caves.

"Selena, talk to me," my mother implores, her voice edged with panic now. "Are you sick again? Is it coming back?"

Oh. *Oh* maybe that's what I should tell them. That they retrieved me too soon. That I need to go back for more treatments. And then Bryxan and I could run away so they can't tear us apart again.

Or maybe I should tell the truth.

"Mother," I say, finally unlocking the door and stepping out into the hall, my expression serene despite the storm raging within. "We need to talk."

My mother takes one look at my face, her own draining of color. She's always been good at reading me. "What's wrong?" she asks, her voice shaky.

"I need to go back," I say steadily, meeting her anxious gaze with determination.

"Back? To the cave?" she stammers out, disbelief in her eyes. "Why would you...?"

"I'm pregnant," I interrupt her, the words tumbling out of my mouth before fear can trap them in my throat. Her mouth drops open in shock.

"Pregnant?" she echoes, her hand flying to her chest, but I see something else flicker in her eyes. Understanding. Slowly, the shock on her face gives way to painful realization. "Oh, Selena..." she murmurs, reaching out to me, and I let her pull me into an embrace.

"Did he hurt you? The orc?"

"No, Mother," I answer quickly, a surge of protectiveness for Bryxan rising within me. "He didn't hurt me. He protected me...cared for me." I pause, taking a deep breath. "And he loves me."

Her arms tighten around me reflexively at my words. "Selena, do you love him?"

"I do. I love him, and I want this baby. I want to go back to be with him."

"You can't mean that. When we sent you there, your father and I were out of our minds. It never should have happened. The unorthodox treatments..."

"I never thought I would have a baby, Mom. Not after I was so sick for so long. I didn't think I would even live much longer. But I'm healthy again. And pregnant. And in love.

Her grip on me slackens. "Selena..." she hesitates, struggling to find the right words, "You've been through so much. Your father and I, we just want what's best for you."

"I know," I whisper, the tears welling up in my eyes. But I force them back, straighten my spine and look my mother in the eye. "And what's best for me is Bryxan."

An uncomfortable silence stretches between us. She looks at me, her maternal instincts warring with her societal programming, wrestling with the reality of my confession. "We...we need to talk to your father," she finally. I nod, knowing the battle isn't over yet.

We find my father in his chair in the living room, reading the paper. He looks up as we enter, eyes moving from my mother's grave expression to my determined one. "What's going on?" he asks.

"Selena wants to go back to the cave."

"Preposterous!" he splutters, jumping up from his chair. "You can't possibly mean that!"

"I do," I say firmly, meeting his incredulous gaze.

"And she's carrying... the creature's child," Mother adds softly.

They argue about me like I'm not there, so I go to the window and tune out. They can't stop me from trying to find him. I'll do it on my own if I have to. Bryxan deserves to know.

The air shivers with a charge that raises the fine hairs on my arms. Something shifts in the atmosphere, like the prelude to a storm. I pull back the curtain. There he stands at the edge of the manicured lawn, an imposing figure that seems to pull the very earth beneath him toward his gravity.

Bryxan.

His warrior dress clings to his massive frame, every piece of armor a testament to the battles he's fought, the victories he's claimed. I'd only ever seen him in simple trousers or a loincloth.

He's here to do battle if he has to.

"Selena?" My mother's voice slices through room. "What are you looking at?"

"Selena, who is that man?" she asks, getting closer to the window.

"He's not a man, Mama. He's an orc. He's my orc. His name is Bryxan," I reply, my voice stronger than I feel. "And he's come for me."

THE FRONT DOOR CRASHES open, and he stands there—fierce and proud. I'm rooted to the spot, breath catching as my eyes trace the contours of his formidable frame.

He steps forward, the ground trembling beneath his weight.

"Selena," he growls, his deep voice resonating through the still air. It's a sound that commands attention, a timbre that speaks of ancient forests and untamed lands. My name on his lips is a declaration, a possessive note that sends a shiver skittering down my spine.

His stride is determined, closing the distance between us with purposeful, heavy steps. There's no room for doubt or hesitation in his manner. His approach is relentless, a predator honing in on its prey. And I realize then, with a thrill, that I'm his quarry.

"Selena," he repeats when he's standing in front of me.

Without another word, he picks me up, one firm hand splayed across my back, the other cradling my knees. He carries me outside despite my parents' worried shouts behind us. The world tilts, and a dizzy rush fills my head as we step through a shimmering portal that materializes before us.

The air changes, charged with the electricity of the unknown. One minute we're on my dad's lawn, the next, we emerge into a forest, one different from the one where we met. The trees are strange, their trunks twisted into unimaginable shapes, their leaves shimmering with an ethereal glow. A faint, warm breeze carrying hints of strange, exotic flowers swirls around us.

And unless I have double vision, there appear to be two suns.

His stride doesn't falter as he carries me deeper into the green embrace of this new world. My gaze locks onto his fierce profile; the set jaw and the taut lines of concentration speak of his relentless determination.

"Where are you taking me?" I ask, not really caring so much because I'm just so happy to be with him. Even though he is acting very, very grumpy.

He grunts, a vow laden with unspoken intentions. His pace never wavers, his muscles flexing beneath the weight of his armor and my form pressed against him.

The path narrows, and Bryxan's surefooted steps lead us into the yawning maw of a cave that seems to breathe with ancient whispers. Shadows dance along the jagged walls, playing tricks on my eyes as I peer into the darkness.

"Where are we?"

"Home," he replies, the single word echoing off the stone, filling the space with the weight of his claim. "Bryxan homeland."

The cave's interior is an intricate network of tunnels and chambers that seem to pulse with a life of their own. Stalactites and stalagmites form a natural architecture of strange beauty. Each step takes us deeper into the heart of it. We come upon a room that reminds me of our sleeping quarters in the other cave, except...that's a real bed. A rough hewn one. An extra, extra large one. But it's a bed.

"Bryxan breed Selena here." His declaration is devoid of romance, but thrums with raw power. "Selena mine. Forever. Will take seed over and over. No escape."

I'm here for it. I like his barbaric show of dominance. But at the same time, my inner feminist bristles with annoyance.

He sets me on the soft furs and begins removing his armor. He is every inch the warrior, his gaze alight with fierce possessiveness. It should scare me. But it doesn't.

"How did we travel here?"

"Portal."

"I don't know what a portal is. I've never seen one."

He grunts. "Selena save strength for fucking. Talk later."

A creature with such huge balls should realize they are also a big target for my foot.

I watch as his rough hands work to unfasten his chest plate, exposing the solid expanse of his torso beneath. The dim light casts hard shadows over his muscles, highlighting the power and strength that radiates from him. When he's completely naked, his cock already hard and ready, he leans over me, his large hands on either side of my head, and sniffs me. "Selena not weak. Not sick. Orc seed make well?"

My heart skips a beat at the tenderness seeping into his voice, his rough features softening.

"Yes," I whisper, reaching up to cradle his face. "You healed me. You also *stole* me."

Dark humor dances in his eyes. "Bryxan not steal, Bryxan claim."

"Whatever. What happens now?"

"Breed little human. Make many fine orc babies." He growls and rips my clothes away from my body. "Selena take orc cock deep in tiny human cunt. Feel orc seed fill womb. No escape."

He positions himself between my legs, spreading them wider with a firm push. His cock rubs against my entrance, the head slippery and warm. I gasp at the contact, my back arching off the ground, my body already so desperate for him. There's a moment of anticipation, as we both stare into each other's eyes, and then he pushes in.

His size stretches me, fills me to the brink. It should hurt, but it doesn't.

The pleasure is unbearable, radiating from the inside out, and I moan loudly. His large hands move to my hips, holding me steady as he begins to thrust. The rhythm is slow at first, gentle even, but escalates quickly as his patience wears thin. A particularly deep thrust sends stars dancing before my eyes. The pleasure is relentless, overwhelming.

"Too much!" I cry out, clutching at his arms.

But Bryxan only smiles down at me, his teeth a sharp contrast to his green skin. "Bryxan not stop," he says, his voice rumbling like thunder, "not until Selena full of orc seed."

He pulls my legs up so my feet rest high on his shoulders, changing the angle of his thrusts. Deeper, harder. Heat builds within me, an inferno that's threatening to consume me whole.

"Bryxan," I gasp his name as he continues to drive into me.

"Selena squeeze Bryxan too good." Sweat beads on his green skin, muscular body straining against the effort of restraining his own pleasure. His rhythm becomes erratic, his thrusts more desperate.

His hand slides down my belly, his fingers finding my clit. A jolt runs through me as he starts to rub it in time with his thrusts, and it doesn't take long for me to reach my limit.

"I'm going to—" The words barely leave my lips before I'm climaxing around him, my cries of ecstasy echoing off the cave walls. His thrusts don't stop, riding me through my orgasm, driving me higher and higher.

"Mine," he grunts, and I can feel his cock swell inside me. He thrusts hard, once, twice more and then he's freezing above me, his eyes locked onto mine as he lets out a guttural roar of his own release. I feel him fill me, hot and thick, a satisfying sensation deep inside.

He slumps down onto me, his heavy body pressing me into the furs beneath us. I wrap my arms around his sweaty back, holding him close. His deep breaths echo in my ear as he slowly comes down from his high, the trembling of his body gradually subsiding.

He rolls us so that I'm laying on him instead.

"You didn't just get me pregnant, you know," I tell him with a sassy tone.

"Bryxan sure."

"I don't think so." I take one of his large hands and place it on my belly. "I was already pregnant."

Surprised, Bryxan raises his body on his elbows, looking down at me. He has an unreadable expression on his rugged features. His eye twitches slightly and he growls, "Selena trick Bryxan."

"Not trick.. surprise," I say, nestling into the crook of his arm. My fingers exploring the rough texture of his skin. "I had just told my parents I was pregnant with your baby and wanted to go back to the cave to find you when you materialized in the yard."

His gaze softens at my words, his hand gently stroking the swell of my belly. "Bryxan no know," he admits, a touch of guilt in his low voice. He turns me gently so we are facing each other properly, his eyes looking deeply into mine. "If Bryxan know Selena want, Bryxan come. No need to take."

"I like being claimed by you. It's sexy."

He rumbles a laugh, tusks glinting in the dim light. "Bryxan promise claim Selena every day."

"Selena promise to claim Bryxan every day."

He pretends to think about it, then nods sagely. "Bryxan like."

Epilogue
Ten months later...

DAWN'S FIRST LIGHT filters through the mouth of the cave, casting a warm glow on our makeshift nest. I blink away the remnants of sleep, stretching my limbs beneath the fur blanket that Bryxan and I share. His arm rests heavily across my waist, a protective barrier even in slumber. Beside me, our baby lies swaddled, a serene expression gracing her tiny face. She's our little miracle, a perfect blend of two worlds. My heart swells with a love so fierce it could outshine the twin suns of this realm.

I ease Bryxan's arm off me, careful not to disturb the delicate balance of our family's rest. His breath hitches momentarily before settling into its steady pace again. I watch him for a moment longer, tracing the lines of his orcish features softened by sleep.

My feet find the cool stone floor without a sound, and I pad silently toward an exit near our sleeping quarters. The air outside holds the fresh promise of a new day, and the terrain stretches in front of me, a wild tapestry of ancient trees and plants that still look foreign to me. Just a short distance away, the stream murmurs its ceaseless song.

I crouch beside the flowing water, dipping my hands in. Its icy touch jolts me awake, washing away the remnants of dreams and the fatigue of motherhood. I scoop handfuls to rinse away the night's sweat and the dust of the cave.

Back at the cave, I move quietly, not wanting to disturb this tranquil tableau, as I gather the supplies we've collected—dried fruits, nuts, some roots that I've learned are both nutritious and pleasantly earthy to the taste.

With practiced hands, I prepare our breakfast, the simplicity of the task grounding me further into this life we've carved out. The soft coos of the baby waking will soon turn to not-so-soft coos, so I wipe my hands and start over to her.

Byxan yawns. "Selena feed Lydia. Bryxan finish breakfast."

Yes, we named our daughter after the internet witch who brought us together. Weird? Maybe.

I get back into bed, and he brings our baby to me to nurse. Lydia's small hands flail as I guide her to my breast, her mouth instantly seeking nourishment. She's green with her father's black eyes and tongue. But she has no tusks, and she has my dimples and chin.

Tomorrow, my parents are meeting her for the first time. We're meeting in a different realm. Not here. Not Earth. Bryxan doesn't trust them yet. Not after they stole me the first time.

I have already met some of Bryxan's family. They didn't believe in humans any more than I believed in orcs last year. But we're finding our way.

After breakfast, we go outside. Bryxan brings his book as he's learning how to read the human word, and I bring my Sudoku and a pencil. We make trips through the portal to Earth regularly for supplies that make me feel more at home, like Sudoku magazines. But I like the simple life we have created here.

As I watch Bryxan, trying to decipher the shapes and sounds of my language, his concentration is endearing. His fingertips trace the lines of text as he fights to make the symbols make sense. I'm struck with a sudden love for him that is deeper than before, if that's even possible. He is learning for me, for Lydia, for us.

And because he likes a good challenge.

When we finish our morning routine, Bryxan takes Lydia in his arms, and I watch as he speaks to her softly. Their bond was strong and immediate. She doesn't cry when he takes her away from me, but rather watches the world from over his enormous shoulder with wide eyes. He takes her inside for a nap and I follow them. As soon as she's asleep, he tackles me on the bed. "Selena need seed."

"Oh really?"

"Hungry for it."

"I am?" I giggle.

Bryxan growls, his low voice vibrating the air between us. "Am see in eyes. Always hungry," he says, his hands roaming my body, tracing the lines and curves that are so familiar to him now.

"I think maybe Bryxan is hungry for Selena," I tell him, playfully.

"Lydia want brother."

I giggle at his logic. "And just how did she tell you that?"

Bryxan grins, tusks protruding in that endearing way they do when he's amused. "Lydia not talk yet. But Bryxan feel it."

"What about a sister?" I suggest.

"Either way, am ready to make one," he purrs, his voice low and laced with teasing promise.

"Well then, orc, come claim your bride."

About the Author

Unfailingly filthy...and super sweet

Brill's books are filthy/sweet for when you're in the mood for something a little over the top. Okay, a lot over the top. Sorry, not sorry.

Brill Harper is represented by Deidre Knight of The Knight Agency.

www.ingramcontent.com/pod-product-compliance
Lightning Source LLC
Chambersburg PA
CBHW031739150726
47989CB00006B/2530